The Vampire

I am a vampire, and that is the truth. But the modern meaning of the word *vampire,* the stories that have been told about creatures such as I, are not precisely true. I do not turn to ash in the sun, nor do I cringe when I see a crucifix. I wear a tiny gold cross around my neck now, but only because I like it. I cannot command a pack of wolves to attack or fly through the air. Nor can I make another of my kind simply by having him drink my blood. Wolves do like me, though, as do most predators, and I can jump so high that one might imagine I can fly. As to blood—ah, blood, the whole subject fascinates me. I do like that, warm and dripping, when I am thirsty. And I am often thirsty. . . .

Books by Christopher Pike

Available from ARCHWAY Paperbacks

Christopher Pike

The Last Vampire

AN ARCHWAY PAPERBACK
Published by POCKET BOOKS
New York London Toronto Sydney Tokyo Singapore

AN ARCHWAY PAPERBACK *Original*

An Archway Paperback published by
POCKET BOOKS, a division of Simon & Schuster Inc.
1230 Avenue of the Americas, New York, NY 10020

ISBN: 0-671-87264-8

First Archway Paperback printing May 1994

10 9 8 7 6 5 4 3 2 1

AN ARCHWAY PAPERBACK and colophon are registered trademarks of Simon & Schuster Inc.

Cover art by Brian Kotzky

Printed in the U.S.A.

IL 9+

For Dr. Pat

The Last Vampire

1

I am a vampire, and that is the truth. But the modern meaning of the word *vampire*, the stories that have been told about creatures such as I, are not precisely true. I do not turn to ash in the sun, nor do I cringe when I see a crucifix. I wear a tiny gold cross now around my neck, but only because I like it. I cannot command a pack of wolves to attack or fly through the air. Nor can I make another of my kind simply by having him drink my blood. Wolves do like me, though, as do most predators, and I can jump so high that one might imagine I can fly. As to blood—ah, blood, the whole subject fascinates me. I do like that as well, warm and dripping, when I am thirsty. And I am often thirsty.

My name, at present, is Alisa Perne—just two words, something to last for a couple of decades. I am no more attached to them than to the sound of the wind. My hair is blond and silklike, my eyes like sapphires that have stared long at a volcanic fissure. My stature is slight by modern standards, five two in sandals, but my arms and legs are muscled, although not unattractively so. Before I speak I appear to be only eighteen years of age, but something in my voice—the coolness of my expressions, the echo of endless experience—makes people think I am much older. But even I seldom think about when I was born, long before the pyramids were erected beneath the pale moon. I was there, in that desert in those days, even though I am not originally from that part of the world.

Do I need blood to survive? Am I immortal? After all this time, I still don't know. I drink blood because I crave it. But I can eat normal food as well, and digest it. I need food as much as any other man or woman. I am a living, breathing creature. My heart beats—I can hear it now, like thunder in my ears. My hearing is very sensitive, as is my sight. I can hear a dry leaf break off a branch a mile away, and I can clearly see the craters on the moon without a telescope. Both senses have grown more acute as I get older.

My immune system is impregnable, my regenerative system miraculous, if you believe in miracles—which I don't. I can be stabbed in the arm with a knife and heal within minutes without scarring. But if I were to be stabbed in the heart, say with the currently fashionable wooden stake, then maybe I would die. It is difficult for even a vampire's flesh to heal around an implanted blade. But it is not something I have experimented with.

But who would stab me? Who would get the chance? I have the strength of five men, the reflexes of the mother of all cats. There is not a system of physical attack and defense of which I am not a master. A dozen black belts could corner me in a dark alley, and I could make a dress fit for a vampire out of the sashes that hold their fighting jackets closed. And I do love to fight, it is true, almost as much as I love to kill. Yet I kill less and less as the years go by because the need is not there, and the ramifications of murder in modern society are complex and a waste of my precious but endless time. Some loves have to be given up, others have to be forgotten. Strange as it may sound, if you think of me as a monster, but I can love most passionately. I do not think of myself as evil.

Why am I talking about all this? Who am I talking to? I send out these words, these thoughts, simply because it is time. Time for what, I do not know, and it does not matter because it is what I want and that is always reason enough for me. My wants—how few they are, and yet how deep they burn. I will not tell you, at present, who I am talking to.

The moment is pregnant with mystery, even for me. I stand outside the door of Detective Michael Riley's office. The hour is late; he is in his private office in the back, the light down low—I know this without seeing. The good Mr. Riley called me three hours ago to tell me I had to come to his office to have a little talk about some things I might find of interest. There was a note of threat in his voice, and more. I can sense emotions, although I cannot read minds. I am curious as I stand in this cramped and stale hallway. I am also annoyed, and that doesn't bode well for Mr. Riley. I knock lightly on the door to his outer office and open it before he can respond.

"Hello," I say. I do not sound dangerous—I am, after all, supposed to be a teenager. I stand beside the secretary's unhappy desk, imagining that her last few paychecks have been promised to her as "practically in the mail." Mr. Riley is at his desk, inside his office, and stands as he notices me. He has on a rumpled brown sport coat, and in a glance I see the weighty bulge of a revolver beneath his left breast. Mr. Riley thinks I am dangerous, I note, and my curiosity goes up a notch. But I'm not afraid he knows what I really am, or he would not have chosen to meet with me at all, even in broad daylight.

"Alisa Perne?" he says. His tone is uneasy.

"Yes."

He gestures from twenty feet away. "Please come in and have a seat."

I enter his office but do not take the offered chair in front of his desk, but rather, one against the right wall. I want a straight line to him if he tries to pull a gun on me. If he does try, he will die, and maybe painfully.

He looks at me, trying to size me up, and it is difficult for him because I just sit here. He, however, is a montage of many impressions. His coat is not only wrinkled but stained—greasy burgers eaten hastily. I note it all. His eyes are red rimmed, from a drug as much as fatigue. I hypothesize his poison to be speed—medicine to nourish long hours beating the pavement. After me? Surely. There is also a glint of satisfaction in his eyes, a prey finally caught. I smile privately at the thought, yet a thread of uneasiness enters me as well. The office is stuffy, slightly chilly. I have never liked the cold, although I could survive an Arctic winter night naked to the bone.

"I guess you wonder why I wanted to talk to you so urgently," he says.

I nod. My legs are uncrossed, my white slacks hanging loose. One hand rests in my lap, the other plays with my hair. Left-handed, right-handed—I am neither, and both.

"May I call you Alisa?" he asks.

"You may call me what you wish, Mr. Riley."

My voice startles him, just a little, and it is the effect I want. I could have pitched it like any modern teenager, but I have allowed my past to enter, the power of it. I want to keep Mr. Riley nervous, for nervous people say much that they later regret.

"Call me Mike," he says. "Did you have trouble finding the place?"

"No."

"Can I get you anything? Coffee? A soda?"

5

"No."

He glances at a folder on his desk, flips it open. He clears his throat, and again I hear his tiredness, as well as his fear. But is he afraid of me? I am not sure. Besides the gun under his coat, he has another beneath some papers at the other side of his desk. I smell the gunpowder in the bullets, the cold steel. A lot of firepower to meet a teenage girl. I hear a faint scratch of moving metal and plastic. He is taping the conversation.

"First off I should tell you who I am," he says. "As I said on the phone, I am a private detective. My business is my own—I work entirely freelance. People come to me to find loved ones, to research risky investments, to provide protection, when necessary, and to get hard-to-find background information on certain individuals."

I smile. "And to spy."

He blinks. "I do not spy, Miss Perne."

"Really." My smile broadens. I lean forward, the tops of my breasts visible at the open neck of my black silk blouse. "It is late, Mr. Riley. Tell me what you want."

He shakes his head. "You have a lot of confidence for a kid."

"And you have a lot of nerve for a down-on-his-luck private dick."

He doesn't like that. He taps the open folder on his desk. "I have been researching you for the last few months, Miss Perne, ever since you moved to Mayfair.

You have an intriguing past, as well as many investments. But I'm sure you know that."

"Really."

"Before I begin, may I ask how old you are?"

"You may ask."

"How old are you?"

"It's none of your business."

He smiles. He thinks he has scored a point. He does not realize that I am already considering how he should die, although I still hope to avoid such an extreme measure. Never ask a vampire her age. We don't like that question. It's very impolite. Mr. Riley clears his throat again, and I think that maybe I will strangle him.

"Prior to moving to Mayfair," he says, "you lived in Los Angeles—in Beverly Hills in fact—at Two-Five-Six Grove Street. Your home was a four-thousand-square-foot mansion, with two swimming pools, a tennis court, a sauna, and a small observatory. The property is valued at six-point-five million. To this day you are listed as the sole owner, Miss Perne."

"It's not a crime to be rich."

"You are not just rich. You are very rich. My research indicates that you own five separate estates scattered across this country. Further research tells me that you probably own as much if not more property in Europe and the Far East. Your stock and bond assets are vast—in the hundreds of millions. But what none of my research has uncovered is how you came across this incredible wealth. There is no record of a family anywhere, and believe me, Miss Perne, I have looked far and wide."

"I believe you. Tell me, whom did you contact to gather this information?"

He enjoys that he has my interest. "My sources are of course confidential."

"Of course." I stare at him; my stare is very powerful. Sometimes, if I am not careful, and I stare too long at a flower, it shrivels and dies. Mr. Riley loses his smile and shifts uneasily. "Why are you researching me?"

"You admit that my facts are accurate?" he asks.

"Do you need my assurances?" I pause, my eyes still on him. Sweat glistens on his forehead. "Why the research?"

He blinks and turns away with effort. He dabs at the perspiration on his head. "Because you fascinate me," he says. "I think to myself, here is one of the wealthiest women in the world, and no one knows who she is. Plus she can't be more than twenty-five years old, and she has no family. It makes me wonder."

"What do you wonder, Mr. Riley?"

He ventures a swift glance at me; he really does not like to look at me, even though I am very beautiful. "Why you go to such extremes to remain invisible," he says.

"It also makes you wonder if I would pay to stay invisible," I say.

He acts surprised. "I didn't say that."

"How much do you want?"

My question stuns him, yet pleases him. He does not have to be the first to dirty his hands. What he does not realize is that blood stains deeper than dirt, and that the stains last much longer. Yes, I think again, he may not have that long to live.

"How much are you offering?" he ventures.

I shrug. "It depends."

"On what?"

"On whether you tell me who pointed you in my direction."

He is indignant. "I assure you that I needed no one to point me in your direction. I discovered your interesting qualities all by myself."

He is lying, of that I am positive. I can always tell when a person lies, almost always. Only remarkable people can fool me, and then they have to be lucky. But I do not like to be fooled—so one has to wonder at even their luck.

"Then my offer is nothing," I say.

He straightens. He believes he is ready to pounce. "Then my counteroffer, Miss Perne, is to make what I have discovered public knowledge." He pauses. "What do you think of that?"

"It will never happen."

He smiles. "You don't think so?"

I smile. "You would die before that happened."

He laughs. "You would take a contract out on my life?"

"Something to that effect."

9

He stops laughing, now deadly serious, now that we are talking about death. Yet I keep my smile since death amuses me. He points a finger at me.

"You can be sure that if anything happened to me the police would be at your door the same day," he says.

"You have arranged to send my records to someone else," I say. "Just in case something should happen to you?"

"Something to that effect." He is trying to be witty. He is also lying. I slide back farther into my chair. He thinks I am relaxing, but I position myself so that my legs are straight out. If I am to strike, I have decided, it will be with my right foot.

"Mr. Riley," I say. "We should not argue. You want something from me, and I want something from you. I am prepared to pay you a million dollars, to be deposited in whatever account you wish, in whatever part of the world you desire, if you will tell me who made you aware of me."

He looks me straight in the eye, tries to, and surely he feels the heat building up inside me because he flinches before he speaks. His voice comes out uneven and confused. He does not understand why I am suddenly so intimidating.

"No one is interested in you except me," he says.

I sigh. "You are armed, Mr. Riley."

"I am?"

I harden my voice. "You have a gun under your coat. You have a gun on your desk under those papers.

10

You are taping this conversation. Now, one might think these are all standard blackmail precautions, but I don't think so. I am a young woman. I don't look dangerous. But someone has told you that I am more dangerous than I look and that I am to be treated with extreme caution. And you know that that someone is right." I pause. "Who is that someone, Mr. Riley?"

He shakes his head. He is looking at me in a new light, and he doesn't like what he sees. My eyes continue to bore into him. A splinter of fear has entered his mind.

"H-how do you know all these things?" he asks.

"You admit my facts are accurate?" I mimic him.

He shakes his head again.

Now I allow my voice to change, to deepen, to resonate with the fullness of my incredibly long life. The effect on him is pronounced; he shakes visibly, as if he is suddenly aware that he is sitting next to a monster. But I am not just any monster. I am a vampire, and in many ways, for his sake, that may be the worst monster of all.

"Someone has hired you to research me," I say. "I know that for a fact. Please don't deny it again, or you will make me angry. I really am uncontrollable when I am angry. I do things I later regret, and I would regret killing you, Mr. Riley—but not for long." I pause. "Now, for the last time, tell me who sent you after me, and I will give you a million dollars and let you walk out of here alive."

He stares at me incredulously. His eyes see one

thing and his ears hear another, I know. He sees a pretty blond girl with startlingly blue eyes, and he hears the velvety voice of a succubus from hell. It is too much for him. He begins to stammer.

"Miss Perne," he begins. "You misunderstand me. I mean you no harm. I just want to complete a simple business deal with you. No one has to . . . get hurt."

I take in a long, slow breath. I need air, but I can hold my breath for over an hour if I must. Yet now I let out the breath before speaking again, and the room cools even more. And Mr. Riley shivers.

"Answer my question," I say simply.

He coughs. "There is no one else."

"You'd better reach for your gun."

"Pardon?"

"You are going to die now. I assume you prefer to die fighting."

"Miss Perne—"

"I am five thousand years old."

He blinks. "What?"

I give him my full, uncloaked gaze, which I have used in the past—alone—to kill. "I am a vampire," I say softly. "And you have pissed me off."

He believes me. Suddenly he believes every horror story he has been told since he was a little boy. That they were all true: the dead things hungering for the warm living flesh; the bony hand coming out of the closet in the black of night; the monsters from another page of reality, the unturned page—who could look so human, so cute.

He reaches for his gun. Too slowly, much too.

I shove myself out of my chair with such force that I am momentarily airborne. My senses switch into a hyper-accelerated mode. Over the last few thousand years, whenever I am threatened, I have developed the ability to view events in extreme slow motion. But this does not mean that I slow down; quite the opposite. Mr. Riley sees nothing but a blur flying toward him. He does not see that as I'm moving. I have cocked my leg to deliver a devastating blow.

My right foot lashes out. My heel catches him in the center of the breastbone. I hear the bones crack as he topples backward onto the floor, his weapon still holstered inside his coat. Although I moved toward him in a horizontal position, I land smoothly on my feet. He sprawls on the floor at my feet beside his overturned chair. Gasping for breath, blood pouring out of his mouth. I have crushed the walls of his heart as well as the bones of his chest, and he is going to die. But not just yet. I kneel beside him and gently put my hand on his head. Love often flows through me for my victims.

"Mike," I say gently. "You would not listen to me."

He is having trouble breathing. He drowns in his own blood—I hear it gurgling deep in his lungs—and I am tempted to put my lips to his and suck it away for him. Such a temptation, to sate my thirst. Yet I leave him alone.

"Who?" he gasps at me.

I continue to stroke his head. "I told you the truth. I

am a vampire. You never stood a chance against me. It's not fair, but it is the way it is." I lean close to his mouth, whisper in his ear. "Now tell me the truth and I will stop your pain. Who sent you after me?"

He stares at me with wide eyes. "Slim," he whispers.

"Who is Slim? A man?"

"Yes."

"Very good, Mike. How do you contact him?"

"No."

"Yes." I caress his cheek. "Where is this Slim?"

He begins to cry. The tears, the blood—they make a pitiful combination. His whole body trembles. "I don't want to die," he moans. "My boy."

"Tell me about Slim and I will take care of your boy," I say. My nature is kind, deep inside. I could have said if you don't tell me about Slim, I will find your dear boy and slowly peel off his skin. But Riley is in too much pain to hear me, and I immediately regret striking so swiftly, not slowly torturing the truth out of him. I did tell him that I was impulsive when I'm angry, and it is true.

"Help me," he pleads, choking.

"I'm sorry. I can only kill, I cannot heal, and you are too badly hurt." I sit back on my heels and glance around the office. I see on the desktop a picture of Mr. Riley posed beside a handsome boy of approximately eighteen. Removing my right hand from Mr. Riley, I reach for the picture and show it to him. "Is this your son?" I ask innocently.

Terror consumes his features. "No!" he cries.

I lean close once more. "I am not going to hurt him. I only want this Slim. Where is he?"

A spasm of pain grips Riley, a convulsion—his legs shake off the floor like two wooden sticks moved by a poltergeist. I grab him, trying to settle him down, but I am too late. His grimacing teeth tear into his lower lip, and more blood messes his face. He draws in a breath that is more a shovel of mud on his coffin. He makes a series of sick wet sounds. Then his eyes roll back in his head, and he goes limp in my arms. Studying the picture of the boy, I reach over and close Mr. Michael Riley's eyes.

The boy has a nice smile, I note.

Must have taken after his mother.

Now my situation is more complicated than when I arrived at the detective's office. I know someone is after me, and I have destroyed my main lead to him or her. Quickly I go through Riley's desk and fail to find anything that promises to be a lead, other than Riley's home address. The reason is sitting behind the desk as I search. Riley has a computer and there is little doubt in my mind that he stored his most important records on the machine. My suspicion is further confirmed when I switch on the computer and it immediately asks for an access code. Even though I know a great deal about computers, more than most experts in the field, I doubt I can get into his data banks without outside help. I pick up the picture of father and son again. They are posed beside a computer. Riley Junior, I suspect, must know the access code. I decide to have a talk with him.

After I dispose of his father's body. My exercise in cleanup is simplified by the fact that Riley has no carpet on his office floor. A brief search of the office building leads me to a closet filled with janitorial supplies. Mop and pail and bucket in hand, I return to Mr. Riley's office and do the job his secretary probably resented doing. I have with me—from the closet —two big green plastic bags, and I slip Riley into them. Before I leave with my sagging burden, I wipe away every fingerprint I have created. There isn't a spot I have touched that I don't remember.

The late hour is such a friend; it has been for so many years. There is not a soul around as I carry Riley downstairs and dump him in my trunk. It is good, for I am not in the mood to kill again, and murder, for me, is very much tied to my mood, like making love. Even when it is necessary.

Mayfair is a town on the Oregon coast, chilly this late in autumn, enclosed by pine trees on one side and salt water on the other. Driving away from Riley's office, I feel no desire to go to the beach, to wade out beyond the surf to sink the detective in deep water. I head for the hills instead. The burial is a first for me in this area. I have killed no one since moving to Mayfair a few months earlier. I park at the end of a narrow dirt road and carry Riley over my shoulder deep into the woods. My ears are alert, but if there are mortals in the vicinity, they are all asleep. I carry no shovel with me. I don't need one. My fingers can impale even the hardest soil more surely than the sharpest knife can poke through a man's flesh. Two miles into the woods I drop Riley onto the ground and go down on my hands and knees and begin to dig. Naturally, my clothes get a bit dirty but I have a washing machine and detergent at home. I do not worry. Not about the body ever being found.

But about other things, I am concerned.

Who is Slim?

How did he find me?

How did he know to warn Riley to treat me with caution?

I lay Riley to rest six feet under and cover him over in a matter of minutes without even a whisper of a prayer. Who would I pray to anyway? Krishna? I could not very well tell *him* that I was sorry, although I did tell him that once, after holding the jewel of his life in my bloodthirsty hands while he casually brought to ruin our wild party. No, I think, Krishna would not listen to my prayer, even if it was for the soul of one of my victims. Krishna would just laugh and return to his flute. To the song of life as he called it. But where was the music for those his followers said were already worse than dead? Where was the joy? No, I would not pray to God for Riley.

Not even for Riley's son.

In my home, in my new mansion by the sea, late at night, I stare at the boy's photo and wonder why he is so familiar to me. His brown eyes are enchanting, so wide and innocent, yet as alert as those of a baby owl seen in the light of the full moon. I wonder if in the days to come I will be burying him beside his father. The thought saddens me. I don't know why.

2

I do not need much sleep, two hours at most, which I usually take when the sun is at its brightest. Sunlight does affect me, although it is not the mortal enemy Bram Stoker imagined in his tale of Count Dracula. I read the novel *Dracula* when it first came out, in ten minutes. I have a photographic memory with a hundred percent comprehension. I found the book delicious. Unknown to Mr. Stoker, he got to meet a real vampire when I paid him a visit one dreary English evening in the year 1899. I was very sweet to him. I asked him to autograph my book and gave him a big kiss before I left. I almost drank some of his blood, I was tempted, but I thought it would have ruined any chance he would have had at writing a sequel, which I

19

encouraged him to do. Humans are seldom able to dwell for any length on things that truly terrify them, even though the horror writers of the present think otherwise. But Stoker was a perceptive man; he knew there was something unusual about me. I believe he had a bit of a crush on me.

But the sun, the eternal flame in the sky, it diminishes my powers. During the day, particularly when the sun is straight up, I often feel drowsy, not so tired that I am forced to rest but weary enough that I lose my enthusiasm for things. Also, I am not nearly so quick or strong during the day, although I am still more than a match for any mortal. I do not enjoy the day as much as the night. I love the blurred edges of darker landscapes. Sometimes I dream of visiting Pluto.

Yet the next day I am busy at dawn. First I call the three businessmen responsible for handling my accounts—each located on a different continent—and tell them I am displeased to learn that my finances have been examined. I listen to each protestation of innocence and detect no falsehood in their voices. My admiration for Mr. Riley's detecting abilities climbs a notch. He must have used subtle means to delve into my affairs.

Or else he'd had help.

Of course I know he had help, but I also believe he turned against the man who sent him to find me. When he realized how rich I was, he must have thought that he could score more handsomely by going after me directly. That leads me to suspect that whoever hired Riley does not know the exact details of my life, where I live and such. But I also realize he will notice Riley's disappearance and come looking for whoever killed him. I have time, I believe, but not much. By nature, I prefer to be the hunter, not the hunted. Yes, indeed, I vow, I will kill those who hired Riley as surely as I wiped him from the face of the earth.

I make arrangements, through my American businessman, to be enrolled at Mayfair High that very day. The wheels are set in motion and suddenly I have a new identity. I am Lara Adams, and my guardian, Mrs. Adams, will visit the school with my transcripts and enroll me in as many of Ray Riley's classes as possible. It has not taken me long to learn the son's name. The arm of my influence is as long as the river of blood I have left across history. I will never meet this fake Mrs. Adams, and she will never meet me, unless she should talk about her efforts on Lara's behalf. Then, if that happens, she will never talk again. My associates respect my desire for silence. I pay them for that respect.

That night I am restless, thirsty. How often do I need to drink blood? I begin to crave it after a week's time. If a month goes by I can think of nothing other than my next dripping throat. I also lose some strength if I go too long. But I do not die without it, at least not readily. I have gone for as long as six months without drinking human blood. I only drink animal blood if I am desperate. It is only when I feed from a human that I feel truly satisfied, and I believe it is the life force in the blood that makes me hunger for it more than the physical fluid itself. I do not know how to define the life force except to say that it exists: the feel of the beating heart when I have a person's vein in my mouth; the heat of their desires. The life force in an animal is of a much cruder density. When I suck on a human, it is as if I absorb a portion of the person's essence, their will. It takes a lot of willpower to live for fifty centuries.

Humans do not turn into vampires after I bite them. Nor do they change into one if they drink my blood. Blood that is drunk goes through the digestive tract and is broken down into many parts. I do not know how the legends started that oral exchange could bring about the transformation. I can only make another vampire by exchanging blood with the person, and not just a little blood. My blood has to overwhelm the other person's system before he or she becomes immortal.

Of course, I do not make vampires these days.

I drive south along the coast. I am in Northern California before I stop; it is late. There is a bar off the side of the road, fairly large. I make a smooth entrance. The men look me over, exchange glances with their buddies. The bartender does not ask me for my ID, not after I give him a hard glance. There are many more men than women around. I am searching for a particular type, someone passing through, and I spot a candidate sitting alone in the corner. He is big and burly, unshaven; his warm jacket is not dirty, but there are oil stains that did not come out from the last cleaning. His face is pleasant enough, sitting behind his frosty beer, but a tad lonely. He is a long-distance truck driver, I know the type. I have often drunk from their veins.

I sit down in front of him, and he looks up in surprise. I smile; the expression can disarm as well as alarm, but he is happy to see me. He orders me a beer and we talk. I do not ask if he is married—though it is obvious he is—and he does not bring it up. After a while we leave and he takes me to a motel, although I would have been satisfied with the back of his truck. I tell him as much, but he pats my leg and shakes his head. He is a gentleman. I won't kill him.

It is while he is undressing me that I bite into his neck. The act makes him sigh with pleasure and lean his head back; he is not really sure what I am doing. He stays in that position the whole time I drink, hypnotized with the sensation, which to him feels as if he is being caressed from the inside out—with the tip of my nails. Which to me feels like it always does, sweet and natural, as natural as making love. But I do not have sex with him. Instead, I bite the tip of my own tongue and let a drop of my blood fall onto his wounds. They heal instantly, leaving no scar, and I lay him down to rest. I have drunk a couple pints. He will sleep deep, maybe wake up with a slight headache.

"Forget," I whisper in his ear.

He won't remember me. They seldom do.

The next morning I sit in Mr. Castro's history class. My cream-colored dress is fashionable, on the rich side; the embroidered hem swings four inches above my knees. I have very nice legs and do not mind showing them off. My long wavy blond hair hangs loose on my shoulders. I wear no makeup or jewelry. Ray Riley sits off to my right, and I study him with interest. Class will begin in three minutes.

His face has a depth his father's never imagined. He is cut in the mode of many handsome modern youths, with curly brown hair and a chiseled profile. Yet his inner character pushes through his natural beauty and almost makes a mockery of it. The boy is already more man than boy. It shows in his brown eyes, soft but quick, in his silent pauses, as he takes in what his classmates say. He reflects on it, and either accepts or rejects it, not caring what the others think. He is his own person, Ray Riley, and I like that about him.

He talks to a girl on his right. Her name is Pat, and she is clearly his girlfriend. She is a scrawny thing, but with a smile that lights up whenever she looks at Ray. Her manner is assertive but not pushy, simply full of life. Her hands are always busy, often touching him. I like her as well and wonder if she is going to be an obstacle. For her sake, I hope not. I honestly prefer not to kill young people.

Pat's clothes are simple, a blouse and jeans. I

suspect her family has little money. But Ray is dressed sharp. It makes me think of the million I offered his father.

Ray does not appear upset. Probably his father often disappears for days at a time.

I clear my throat and he looks over at me.

"Hello," he says. "Are you new?"

"Hi," I say. "Yes. I just checked in this morning." I offer my dainty hand. "My name's Lara Adams."

"Ray Riley." He shakes my hand. His touch is warm, his blood healthy. I can smell blood through people's skin and tell if they have any serious ailments —even years before the disease manifests. Ray continues to stare at me, and I bat my long lashes. Behind him Pat has stopped talking to another classmate and looks over. "Where are you from?" he asks.

"Colorado."

"Really? You have a slight accent."

His comment startles me because I am a master at accents. "What accent do you hear?" I ask, genuinely curious.

"I don't know. English, French—it sounds like a combination."

I have lived in both England and France for extended periods of time. "I have traveled a lot," I say. "Maybe that's what you hear."

"Must be." He gestures to his side. "Lara, this is my girlfriend, Pat McQueen. Pat, meet Lara Adams."

Pat nods. "Hi, Lara." Her manner is not the least defensive. She trusts in Ray's love, and in her own.

That is going to change. I think of Riley's computer, which I have left in his office. It will not be terribly long before the police come to look around, and maybe take the computer away. But I have not taken the machine because I would have no way of explaining to Ray what I was doing with it, much less be able to convince him to open its data files.

"Hello, Pat," I say. "Nice to meet you."

"Same here," she says. "That's a beautiful dress."

"Thank you." I would have preferred to have met Ray without Pat around. Then it would have been easier for him to start a relationship with me without her between us. Yet I am confident I can gather Ray's interest. What man could resist what I have to offer? My eyes go back to him. "What are we studying in this class?" I ask.

"European history," he says. "The class just gives a broad overview. Right now we're talking about the French Revolution. Know anything about it?"

"I knew Marie Antoinette personally," I lie. I knew *of* Antoinette, but I was never close to the French nobility, for they were boring. But I was there, in the crowd, the day Marie Antoinette was beheaded. I actually sighed when the blade sliced across her neck. The guillotine was one of the few methods of execution that disturbed me. I have been hanged a couple of times and crucified on four separate occasions, but I got over it. But had I lost my head, I know that would have been the end. I was there at the start of the

French Revolution, but I was in America before it
ended.

"Did she really say, 'Let them eat cake'?" Ray asks,
going along with what he thought was a joke.

"I believe it was her aunt who said that." The
teacher, Mr. Castor, enters the room, a sad-looking
example of a modern educator if ever there was one.
He only smiles at the pretty girls as he strides to the
front of the room. He is attractive in an aftershave-
commercial sort of way. I nod to him. "What's he
like?"

Ray shrugs. "Not bad."

"But not good?"

Ray sizes me up. "I think he'll like you."

"Understood."

The class starts. Mr. Castro introduces me to the
rest of the students and asks me to stand and talk
about myself. I remain seated and say ten words. Mr.
Castor appears put out but lets it go. The lesson
begins.

Ah, history, what an illusion humanity has of the
past. And yet scholars argue the reality of their texts
until they are blue in the face, even though something
as recent as the Second World War is remembered in a
manner that has no feeling for the times. For *feeling,*
not events, is to me the essence of history. The
majority of people recollect World War II as a great
adventure against impossible odds, while it was nothing but an unceasing parade of suffering. How quickly

mortals forget. But I forget nothing. Even I, a blood-thirsty harlot if ever there was one, have never wit-nessed a glorious war.

Mr. Castro has no feeling for the past. He doesn't even have his facts straight. He lectures for thirty minutes, and I grow increasingly bored. The bright sun has me a bit sleepy. He catches me peeking out the window.

"Miss Adams," he says, interrupting my reverie. "Could you give us your thoughts on the French nobility?"

"I think they were very noble," I say.

Mr. Castro frowns. "You approve of their excesses at the expense of the poor?"

I glance at Ray before answering. I do not think he wants the typical teenage girl, not deep inside, and I have no intention of acting like one. He is watching me, the darling boy.

"I don't approve or disapprove," I say. "I accept it. People in power always take advantage of those with-out power."

"That sounds like a generalization if I ever heard one," Mr. Castro replies. "What school did you go to before moving to Mayfair?"

"What school I went to doesn't matter."

"It sounds as if you have a problem with authority," Mr. Castro says.

"Not always. It depends."

"On what?"

"Whether the authority is foolish or not," I say with

a smile that leaves no doubt I am talking about him. Mr. Castro, wisely, passes me over and goes on to another topic.

But the teacher asks me to stay behind when the bell rings. This bothers me; I wish to use this time to speak to Ray. I watch as he leaves the room with Pat. He glances over his shoulder at me just before he goes out of sight. Mr. Castro taps his desk, wanting my attention.

"Is there something wrong?" I ask him.

"I hope not," Mr. Castro says. "I am concerned, however, that we get off to a good start. That each of us understands where the other is coming from."

I stare at him, not strongly enough to cause him to wilt, but enough to make him squirm. "I believe I understand exactly where you're coming from," I say.

He is annoyed. "Oh, and where is that?"

I can smell alcohol on his breath, from the previous night, and alcohol from the night before that, and the night before that. He is only thirty, but the circles under his eyes indicate his liver is close to seventy. His tough stance is only an image; his hands shake as he waits for me to respond. His eyes are all over my body. I decide to ignore his question.

"You think I have a bad attitude," I say. "Honestly, I am not what you think. If you knew me you would appreciate my understanding of history and . . ." I let my voice trail off. "Other things."

"What grade are you hoping to get in this class?"

His question makes me laugh, it is so ridiculous. I

lean over and give his cheek a pinch, a hard one that makes him jump. He's lucky I don't do the same to his crotch. "Why, Mr. Castro, I'm sure you're going to give little old Lara just about any grade she wants, don't you think?"

He tries to brush my hand away, but of course it is already gone. "Hey! You better watch it, miss."

I giggle. "I'll be watching you, Mr. Castro. Just to make sure you don't die of drink before the semester's over. I've got to get that good grade, you know."

"I don't drink," he protests feebly as I walk away.

"And I don't give a damn about my grade," I say over my shoulder.

I fail to catch Ray before my next class starts, which I do not share with him. Seems my pseudo guardian was unable to match my schedule exactly to Ray's. I sit through fifty minutes of trigonometry, which naturally I know almost as well as history. I manage to refrain from alienating the teacher.

The next period I don't have with Ray either, although I know fourth period we will be together in biology. Third is P.E. and I have brought blue shorts and a white T-shirt to wear. The *girlfriend*, Pat McQueen, has the locker beside mine and speaks to me as we undress.

"Why did Castro ask you to stay behind?" she asks.

"He wanted to ask me out."

"He likes the girls, that guy. What did you think of Ray?"

Pat is not excessively paranoid, but she is trying to

ascertain where I am coming from. "I think he needs lots of love," I say.

Pat is not sure what to think of that, so she laughs. "I give him more than he can handle." She pauses, admiring my momentarily naked body. "You know, you really are incredibly beautiful. You must have guys hitting on you all the time."

I pull on my shorts. "I don't mind. I just hit them back. Hard."

Pat smiles, a bit nervously.

Phys ed is currently educating the boys and girls of Mayfair in the rudiments of archery. I am intrigued. The class is coed and the bow and arrow in my hands bring back old memories. Perhaps, though, the ancient memory of Arjuna, Krishna's best friend and the greatest archer of all time, is not one I should stir. For Arjuna killed more vampires than any other mortal.

All with one bow.

All in one night.

All because Krishna wished it so.

Pat follows me out onto the field, but tactfully separates herself from me as we select our equipment. I have already spooked her, and I don't think that is bad. I wear strong sunglasses, gray tinted. As I gather my bow and arrows, an anemic-looking young man with thick glasses and headphones speaks to me.

"You're new, aren't you?" he asks.

"Yes. My name is Lara Adams. Who are you?"

"Seymour Dorsten." He offers his hand. "Pleased to meet you."

My flesh encloses his, and I know instantly that this young man will be dead in less than a year. His blood is sick—how can the rest of his body not be? I hold on to his hand a moment too long, and he stares at me quizzically.

"You are strong," he says.

I smile and let go of him. "For a girl?"

He rubs his hand on his side. His illness has startled me. I have bruised him. "I suppose," he says.

"What kind of name is Seymour? It makes you sound like a nerd."

He likes my forthright manner. "I've always hated it. My mother gave it to me."

"Change it when you get out of high school. Change it to Marlboro or Slade or Bubba or something like that. And lose those glasses. You should be wearing contacts. I bet your mother even buys your clothes."

I am a revelation to Seymour. He laughs. "She does. But since I *am* a nerd, shouldn't I look the part?"

"You think you're a nerd because you think you're so smart. I'm a lot smarter than you and I look great." I gesture to our bows and arrows. "Where should we shoot these things?"

"I think it would be best if we shot them at the targets," he says wisely.

So that's what we do. A few minutes later we are at one end of the football field sending our arrows flying toward the targets that have been arranged in a neat row on the fifty-yard line. I impress Seymour when I hit the bull's-eye three times in a row. He is further impressed when we go to remove the arrows from the target and they are stuck in so deep he has to use all his strength to pull them out. He does not know that I could have split the shaft of my first arrow with the next two if I had wished. I am showing off, I know, and it is probably not the wisest thing to do, but I don't care. My mood this day is frivolous. My first day of high school. First happy thoughts about Ray and Pat and now I have taken an immediate liking to Seymour. I help him pull the arrows from the target.

"You have shot before," he says.

"Yes. I was trained by a master marksman."

He pulls out the last arrow and almost falls to the ground as it comes loose. "You should be in the Olympics."

I shrug as we walk back toward the goal posts. "I have no interest," I say.

Seymour nods. "I feel the same way about mathematics. I'm great at it, but it bores me to death."

"What does interest you?"

"Writing."

"What do you like to write?"

"I don't know yet. The strange and unusual fascinates me." He pauses. "I read a lot of horror books. Do you like horror?"

"Yes." I start to make a joke of his question, something about how close it is to my heart, but a feeling of déjà vu sweeps over me. The feeling startles me, for I haven't had it in centuries. The sensation is intense; I put a hand to my head to steady myself, while searching for the source of it. Seymour reaches out to help, and once more I feel the sickness flowing beneath his skin. I am not sure of the nature of his disease, but I have a good idea what it is.

"Are you all right?" he asks me.

"Yes." A cool film of sweat has gathered on my forehead, and I wipe it away. My sweat is clear, not tinted pink, as it becomes when I drink large quantities of human blood. The sun burns bright in the sky and I lower my head. Seymour continues to watch me. Suddenly I feel as if he has come so close to me his body is actually overlapping mine. Like the déjà vu, I do not like the sensation. I wonder if I have developed a greater sensitivity to the sun. I have not been out like this, at midday, in many years.

"I feel as if I've met you before," he says softly, puzzled.

"I feel the same way," I say honestly, the truth of the matter finally striking me. Already I have said how I can sense emotions, and that is true. The ability came to me slowly as the centuries of my life passed. At first I assumed it was because of my intense observatory faculties, and I still feel that is part of it. Yet I can sense a person's feelings even without studying them closely, and the ability baffles me to this day because it suggests a sense that is nonphysical, which I am not yet ready to accept.

I am not alone with this ability. Over time I have met the occasional human who was as sensitive as I.

Indeed, I have killed several of them because they alone could sense what I was, or rather, what I was not. Not human. Something else, they would tell their friends, something dangerous. I killed them, but I did not want to because they alone could understand me.

I sense now that Seymour is one of these humans. The feeling is further confirmed when once more I pick up my bow and arrow and aim at the target. For my vision is distracted. Mr. Castro stands in the distance behind the school gymnasium, talking to a perky blond. Talking and touching—obviously making a move on the young thing. The teacher is perhaps three hundred yards distant, but for me, with a bow in my strong arms, he is within range. As I toy with my next arrow, I think that I can shoot him in the chest and no one will know—or believe—that it was really me who killed him. I can make it so that even Seymour doesn't see where the arrow flies. Killing Mr. Riley two nights earlier has awakened in me the desire to kill again. Truly, violence does beget violence, at least for a vampire—nothing quite satisfies as does the sight of blood, except for the taste of it.

I slip the arrow into the bow.

My eyes narrow.

Castro strokes the girl's hair.

Yet out of the corner of my eye I notice Seymour watching me.

Seeing what? Sensing what? The blood fever in me? Perhaps. His next word is revealing.

"Don't," he says.

My aim wavers. I am amazed. Seymour knows I am thinking about killing Castro! Who is this Seymour, I ask myself? I lower my bow and look over at him. I have to ask.

"Don't *what?*" I say.

His eyes, magnified behind their glasses, stare at me. "You don't want to shoot anybody."

I laugh out loud, although his remark chills me. "What makes you think I want to shoot somebody?"

He smiles and relaxes a notch. My innocent tone has done its work on him. Perhaps. I wonder if Seymour is one of those rare mortals who can fool even me.

"I just had the feeling you were going to," he says. "I'm sorry."

"Do I look so dangerous?"

He shakes his head. "You are different from anyone I have ever met."

First Ray notices that I have an accent, and now Seymour reads my mind. An interesting day, to say the least. I decide I should keep a lower profile, for the time being.

Yet I do not really believe he has read my mind. If I did, like him or not, I would kill him before the sun set.

"You're just so dazzled by my beauty," I say.

He laughs and nods. "It isn't often a beauty such as you is caught talking to a nerd like me."

I lightly poke him in the belly with the tip of my arrow. "Tell me more about the kind of stories you like." I nock the arrow onto my bowstring. Mr. Castro will live another day, I think, but maybe not many more. I add, "Especially your favorite horror stories."

So for the rest of the period Seymour tells me about an assortment of authors and books he has read. I am delighted to learn that *Dracula* is his all-time favorite story. I miss the bull's-eye a few times on purpose, but I don't know if I fool Seymour. He never takes his eyes off me.

The next period I am off to biology. Ray sits in the back at a lab table. I waste no time. I walk straight back and sit beside him. He raises an eyebrow as if to say that someone else has that seat, but then seems to change his mind.

"How did you enjoy archery?" he asks.

"You talked to Pat?" I ask.

"Yes."

There she is again, the girlfriend, between us. Once more I think of the data files at Mr. Riley's office. If the police do examine them, and do decide Mr. Riley has met with foul play, they will be paying me a visit. If I cannot access the files soon, I will have to destroy them. I decide to hasten things, knowing that I run the risk of destroying my whole seduction. I want to look at those files tonight. I reach over and touch Ray's arm.

"Can you do me a big favor?" I ask.

He glances at my fingertips on his bare arm. My touch is warm. Wait till he feels it hot. "Sure," he says.

"My parents are gone for a few days, and I need some help moving some things into my house. They're in the garage." I add, "I could pay you for your help."

"You don't have to pay me. I'd be glad to help this weekend."

"Actually, one of these *things* is my bed. I had to sleep on the floor last night."

"What a drag." Ray takes a breath and thinks. My hand continues to rest on his arm, and surely the soft texture of my skin must be a part of his thought processes. "I have to work after school today."

"Till what time?"

"Nine. But then I'm supposed to go over and see Pat."

"She's a lovely girl." My eyes rest on his eyes. It is as if they say, yes, lovely, but there are other things in life besides love. At least that is my intention. Yet as I stare into Ray's eyes, I can't help but feel that he is one of those rare mortals I could love. This is another startling revelation for me, and already, even before noon, it seems the day is to be filled with them. I have not loved a man—or a woman for that matter—in centuries. And none have I ever loved as much as my husband, Rama, before I was made into a vampire.

Yet Rama comes to mind as I stare at Ray, and at last I know why Ray looks familiar. He has Rama's eyes.

Ray blinks. "We've been going out for a year."

I sigh unintentionally. Even after fifty centuries I still miss Rama. "A year can pass quickly," I say softly.

But not five thousand—the long years stand behind me like so many ghosts, weary, but also wary. Time sharpens caution, destroys playfulness. I think how nice it would be to go for a walk in the park with Ray, in the dark. I could kiss him, I could bite him— gently. I sigh because this poor boy doesn't know he is sitting beside his father's murderer.

"Maybe I can help you," Ray says clearly. My eyes do not daunt him as much as I would expect, and I do not know if that is because of his own internal strength or because my glance is softened by my affection for him. "But I'll have to check with Pat."

I finally take my hand back. "If you check with Pat, she'll say it is fine to help me as long as she gets to come along." I shrug. "Any girl would."

"Can she come over, too?"

"No."

My answer startles him. But he is too shrewd to ask me why. He simply nods. "I'll talk to her. Maybe I can come a little later. What time do you go to bed?"

"Late."

The lecture in biology is about photosynthesis. How the sun's energy is changed into chemical energy through the presence of green chlorophyll, and how this green pigment in turn supports the entire food chain. The teacher makes a comment I find interest- ing—chlorophyll and red blood cells are practically identical. Except in chlorophyll the iron atom is replaced by a magnesium atom. I look over at Ray and think that in the evolutionary chain, only one atom separates us.

Of course, I know that evolution would never have created a vampire. We were an accident, a horrible mistake. It occurs to me that if Ray does help me examine his father's files, I should probably kill him afterward. He smiles at me as I look at him. I can tell he likes me already. But I don't smile back. My thoughts are too dark.

The class ends. I give Ray my address, but not my phone number. He will not call and cancel on me. It is the address of a new house that was rented for me that morning. Mr. Riley will have my other address in his files, and I don't want Ray to draw the connection when and if we go into his computer. Ray promises to come over as soon as he is able. He does not have sex on his mind, but something else I cannot fathom. Still, I will give him sex if he wants it. I will give him more than he bargains for.

I go to my new home, a plain suburban affair. It is furnished. Quickly, not breaking a sweat, I move most of the furniture into the garage. Then I retire to the master bedroom, draw all the shades, and lie down on the hard wooden floor and close my eyes. The sun has drained my strength, I tell myself. But as I doze off I know it is also the people I have met this day that have cut deep into me, where my iron blood flows like a black river over the cold dust of forgotten ages, dripping onto this green world, onto the present, like the curse of the Lord himself. I hope to dream of Krishna as I fall asleep, but I do not. The devil is there instead.

Yaksha, the first of the vampires.

As I am the last.

3 ~~~

We were the original Aryans—blond and blue eyed.
We invaded India, before there were calendars, like a
swarm of hornets in search of warmer climates. We
brought sharp swords and spilled much blood. But in
3000 B.C., when I was born, we were still there, no
longer enemies, but part of a culture that was capable
of absorbing every invader and making him a brother.
I came into the world named Sita, in a small village in
Rajastan, where the desert had already begun to blow
in sand from the dead lands to the west. I was there at
the beginning, and had as a friend the mother of all
vampires. *Amba*, which meant mother in my lan-
guage. She was a good woman.

Amba was seven years older than my seven years

42

when the disease came to our village. Although separated by seven years, we were good friends. I was tall for my age, she was short, and we both loved to sing, bajans mainly, holy songs from the sacred Vedas, which we chanted by the river after dark. My skin was brown from the harsh sun; Amba's dark from a grandfather who was of original Indian stock. We did not look alike, but when we sang our voices were one and I was happy. Life was simple in Rajastan.

Until the disease came. It did not strike everyone, only half. I do not know why I was spared, since I drank from the polluted river as much as Amba and the rest. Amba was one of the first to fall ill. She vomited blood the last two days of her life, and all I could do was sit by her side and watch her die. My sorrow was particularly great because Amba was eight months pregnant at the time. Even though I was her best friend, she never did tell me who the father was. She never told anyone.

When she died, it should have ended there. Her body should have been taken to the cremation ground and offered to Vishnu, her ashes thrown in the river. But recently an Aghoran priest had entered our village. He had other ideas for her body. Aghora was the left-handed path, the dark path, and no one would have listened to what the priest had to say if the panic over the plague hadn't been in the air. The priest brought his blasphemous ideas, but many listened to him because of their fears for the plague. He said the plague was the result of an evil *rakshasa* or demon

43

that had taken offense at our worship of the great God Vishnu. He said the only way to free our village of the rakshasa was to call forth an even greater being, a *yakshini*, and implore the yakshini to eat the rakshasa.

Some thought this idea was reasonable, but many others, myself included, felt that if God couldn't protect us, how could a yakshini? Also, many of us worried what the yakshini would do once it had devoured the rakshasa. From our Vedic texts we knew that yakshinis had no love for human beings. But the Aghoran priest said that he could handle the yakshini, and so he was allowed to go ahead with his plans.

Aghorans usually do not invoke a deity into a statue or an altar but into the corpse of someone recently dead. It is this practice in particular that has them shunned by most religious people in India. But desperate people often forget their religion when they need it most. There were so many dead at the time, the priest had his choice of corpses. But he chose Amba's body, and I think the fact of her late pregnancy attracted him. I was only a child at the time, but I could see something in the eyes of the priest that frightened me. Something cold and uncaring.

Being so young, I was not permitted to attend the ceremony. None of the women were allowed. Because I was worried what they were going to do with my friend's body, however, I stole into the woods in the middle of the night they were to perform the invocation. I watched from behind a boulder, at the edge of a clearing, as the Aghoran priest with the help of six men—one of them my father—prepared Amba's naked body. They anointed her with clarified butter and camphor and wine. Then, beside a roaring fire, seated close to Amba's upturned head, the priest began a long repetitious chant. I did not like it; it sounded nothing like the bajans we chanted to Vishnu. The mantras were hard on the ear, and each time the priest completed a verse, he would strike Amba's belly with a long sharp stick. It was as if he were imploring her to wake up, or else trying to wake something up inside her.

This went on for a long time, and soon Amba's belly began to bleed, which frightened the men. Because she bled as a living person, as if there were a heart beating inside her. But I knew this could not be. I had been with Amba when she died and sat beside her body for a long time afterward, and not once, even faintly, had she drawn in a breath. I was not tempted to run to her. Not for a moment did I believe the priest had brought her back to life. Indeed, I was tempted to flee back to my mother, who surely must have been wondering where I was. Especially when a dark cloud went over the moon and a heavy breeze began to stir, a wind that stank of decay and waste. The smell was atrocious. It was as if a huge demon had suddenly appeared and breathed down upon the ceremony.

Something had come. As the smell worsened, and the men began to mutter aloud that they should stop, the fire abruptly shrank to red coals. Smoke filled the air, curling around the bloody glow of the embers like so many snakes over a rotting prey. Some of the men cried out in fear. But the priest laughed and chanted louder. Yet even his voice failed when Amba suddenly sat up.

She was hideous to behold. Her face dripped blood. Her eyes bulged from her head as if pushed out from the inside. Her grin widened over her teeth as if pulled by wires. Worst of all was her tongue; it stretched much longer than any human tongue could, almost a foot, curling and licking at the air like the smoking snakes that danced beside what was left of the fire. I watched it in horror knowing that I was seeing a yakshini come to life. In the haunting red glow it turned to face the priest, who had fallen silent. No longer did he appear confident.

The yakshini cackled like a hyena and reached out and grabbed the priest.

The priest screamed. No one came to his aid.

The yakshini pulled the priest close, until they were face to face. Then that awful tongue licked the priest's face, and the poor man's screams gagged in his throat. Because wherever he was touched by the tongue, his skin was pulled away. When the priest was a faceless mass of gore, the yakshini threw its head back and laughed. Then its hands flew up behind the priest's neck and took hold of his skull. With one powerful yank it twisted the priest's head around until it was facing the other way, his bones cracking. The priest fell over dead as the yakshini released him. Then the monster, still seated, glanced around the campfire at the terrified men. A sly glance it was. It smiled as its eyes came to rest on me. Yes, I believe it could see me even as I cowered behind the huge stone that separated me from the clearing. Its eyes felt like cold knives pressing into my heart.

Then finally, thankfully, the monster closed its eyes, and Amba's body lay back down.

For a long moment none of the men moved. Then my father—a brave man, although not the wisest—moved and knelt beside Amba's corpse. He poked it with a stick and it did not move. He poked the priest as well, but it was clear the man wasn't going to be performing any more ceremonies in this life. The other men came up beside my father. There was talk of cremating both of the bodies then and there. Hiding behind my boulder, I nodded vigorously. The stench had blown away on the wind, and I did not want it to return. Unfortunately, before more wood could be gathered, my father noticed movement inside Amba's belly. He cried out to the others. Amba was not dead. Or if she was, he said, her child was not. He reached for a knife to cut the infant out of Amba's womb.

It was then I jumped from behind the boulder and ran into the clearing.

"Father!" I cried, reaching for his hand holding the

knife. "Do not let that child come into this world. Amba is dead, see with your own eyes. Her child must likewise be dead. Please, Father, listen to me."

Naturally, all the men were surprised to see me, never mind hear what I had to say. My father was angry at me, but he knelt and spoke to me patiently.

"Sita," he said. "Your friend does appear dead, and we were wrong to let this priest use her body in this way. But he has paid for his evil karma with his own life. But we would be creating evil karma of our own if we do not try to save the life of this child. You remember when Sashi was born, how her mother died before she came into the world? It sometimes happens that a living child is born to a dead woman."

"No," I protested. "That was different. Sashi was born just as his mother died. Amba has been dead since early dawn. Nothing living can come out of her."

My father gestured with his knife to the squirming life inside Amba's bloody abdomen. "Then how do you explain the life here?"

"That is the yashini moving inside her," I said. "You saw how the demon smiled at us before it departed. It intends to trick us. It is not gone. It has entered into the child."

My father pondered my words with a grave expression. He knew I was intelligent for my age and occasionally asked for my advice. He looked to the other men for guidance, but they were evenly divided. Some wanted to use the knife to stab the life moving inside Amba. Others were afraid, like my father, of committing a sin. Finally my father turned back to me and handed me the knife.

"You knew Amba better than any of us," he said. "You would best know if this life that moves inside her is evil or good. If you know for sure in your heart that it is evil, then strike it dead. None of the men here will blame you for the act."

I was appalled. I was still a child and my father was asking me to commit an atrocious act. But my father was wiser than I had taken him for. He shook his head as I stared at him in amazement, and took back the knife.

"You see," he said. "You are not sure if what you say is true. In a matter of life and death, we must be careful. And if we are to make an error, it must be on the side of life. If this child turns out to be evil, then we will know as it grows up. Then we will have more time to decide what should be done with it." He turned back to Amba's body. "For now I must try to save it."

"We may not have as much time as you think," I said as my father began to cut into Amba's flesh. Soon he held a bloody male infant in his hand. He gave it a gentle spank, and it sucked in a dry rasping breath and began to cry. Most of the men smiled and applauded, although I noticed the fear in their eyes. My father turned to me and asked me to hold it. I refused. However, I did consent to name the child.

"It should be called Yaksha," I said. "For it has the heart of a yakshini."

And the child's name was as I said. Most considered it an evil omen, yet none of them, in their darkest dreams, would realize how appropriate the name would be. But from that time on, the plague vanished and never returned.

My father gave Yaksha to my aunt to raise, for she had no children of her own and greatly desired one. A simple but loving woman, she treated the child as if it were her own—certainly as if it were a human deserving of her love. Whether she felt any love in return from the child, I don't know. He was a beautiful baby with dark hair and pale blue eyes.

Time went by, and it always does, and yet for Yaksha and for me the years took on a peculiar quality. For Yaksha grew faster than any child in the history of our village, and when I was fifteen years of age, he was already, in stature and education, my age, although he had been born only eight years earlier. His accelerated development brought to surface once again the rumors surrounding his birth. But they were rumors at best because the men who had been there the night Yaksha had come into the world never spoke about what had happened when the priest had tried to invoke the yakshini into Amba's corpse. They must have sworn one another to secrecy because my father occasionally took me aside and reminded me that I should not talk about that night. I did not, of course, because I did not think anyone outside of the six men would have believed me. Besides, I loved my father and always tried to obey him, even when I thought he was making a mistake.

It was at about this time, when I was fifteen, that Yaksha started to go out of the way to talk to me. Until then I had avoided him, and even when he pursued me I tried to keep my distance. At least at first, but there was something about him that made him hard to resist. There was his great beauty, of course, his long shiny mane of black hair, his brilliant eyes, cool blue gems, set deep in his powerful face. His smile was also beguiling. How often it flashed in my direction, his two rows of perfect white teeth like polished pearls. Sometimes I would stop to talk to him, and he would always have a little gift to offer—a spoonful of sandlepaste, a stick of incense, a string of beads. I accepted these gifts reluctantly because I felt as if one day Yaksha would want something in return, something I would not want to give. But he never asked.

But my attraction to him went deeper than his beauty. Even at eight years of age he was clearly the smartest person in the village, and often the adults consulted him on important matters: how to improve the harvest; how best to build our new temple; how to barter with the wandering merchants who came to buy our crops. If people had doubts about Yaksha's origin, they had nothing but praise for his behavior.

I was attracted to him, but I never ceased to fear him. Occasionally I would catch a disturbing glimmer in his eyes, and be reminded of the sly smile the yashini had given me before it had supposedly vacated Amba's body.

It was when I was sixteen that the first of the six men who had witnessed his birth disappeared. The man just vanished. Later that same year another of the six disappeared also. I asked my father about it, but he said that we could not hold Yaksha to blame. The boy was growing up well. But the next year, when another two of the men vanished, even my father began to have doubts. It was not long after that my father and I were the only ones left in the village who had been there that horrible night. But the fifth man did not just vanish. His body was found gored to death, as if by a wild animal. There was not a drop of blood left in his corpse. Who could doubt that the others had not ended up the same way?

I begged my father to speak up about what was happening, and Yaksha's part in it. By then Yaksha was ten and looked twenty, and if he was not the leader of the village, few people doubted that he would be in charge soon. But my father was soft-hearted. He had watched Yaksha grow up with pride, no doubt feeling personally responsible for the birth of this wonderful young man. And his sister was still Yaksha's stepmother. He told me not to say anything to the others, that he would ask Yaksha to leave the village quietly and not come back.

But it was my father who was not to come back, although Yaksha vanished as well. My father's body was never found, except for a lock of his hair, down by the river, stained with blood. At the ceremony honoring his death I broke down and cried out the many things that had happened the night Yaksha had been born. But the majority of people believed I was consumed with grief and didn't listen. Still, a few heard me, the families of the other men who had vanished.

My grief over my lost father faded slowly. Yet two years after his death and the disappearance of Yaksha, near my twentieth birthday, I met Rama, the son of a wandering merchant. My love for Rama was instantaneous. I saw him and knew I was supposed to be with him, and by the blessings of Lord Vishnu, he felt the same way. We were married under the full moon beside the river. The first night I slept with my husband I dreamed of Amba. She was as she had been when we had sung late at night together. Yet her words to me were dark. She told me to beware the blood of the dead, never to touch it. I woke up weeping and was only able to sleep by holding my husband tightly.

Soon I was with child, and before the first year of my marriage was over, we had a daughter—Lalita, she who plays. Then my joy was complete and my grief over my father faded. Yet I was to have that joy for only a year.

One moonless night I was awakened late by a sound. Beside me slept my husband, and on my other side our daughter. I do not know why the sound woke me;

it was not loud. But it was peculiar, the sound of nails scraping over a blade. I got up and went outside my house and stood in the dark and looked around.

He came from behind me, as he often used to when we were friends. But I knew he was there before he spoke. I sensed his proximity—his inhuman being.

"Yaksha," I whispered.

"Sita." His voice was very soft.

I whirled around and started to shout, but he was on me before I could make a sound. For the first time I felt Yaksha's real strength, a thing he had kept hidden while he lived in our village. His hands, with their long nails, were like the paws of a tiger around my neck. A long sword banged against his knee. He choked off my air and leaned over and whispered in my ear. He had grown taller since I last saw him.

"You betrayed me, my love," he said. "If I let you speak, will you scream? If you scream you will die. Understood?"

I nodded and he loosened his grip, although he continued to keep me pinned. I had to cough before I could speak. "You betrayed me," I said bitterly. "You killed my father and those other men."

"You do not know that," he said.

"If you didn't kill them, then where are they?"

"They are with me, a few of them, in a special way."

"What are you talking about? You lie—they are dead, my father's dead."

"Your father is dead, that is true, but only because

54

he did not want to join me." He shook me roughly. "Do you wish to join me?"

It was so dark, I could see nothing of his face except in outline. But I did believe he was smiling at me. "No," I said.

"You do not know what I am offering you."

"You are evil."

He slapped me, hard. The blow almost took off my head. I tasted my own blood. "You do not know what I am," he said, angry, but proud as well.

"But I do. I was there that night. Didn't the others tell you before you killed them? I saw it all. It was I who named you—Yaksha—cursed son of a yakshini!"

"Keep your voice down."

"I will do nothing you say!"

He gripped me tight again, and it was hard to breathe. "Then you will die, lovely Sita. After first watching your husband and child die. Yes, I know they are asleep in this house. I have watched you from afar for a while now."

"What do you want?" I gasped, bitter.

He let me go. His tone was light and jovial, which was cruel. "I have come to offer you two choices. You can come with me, be my wife, become *like me.* Or you and your family can die tonight. It is that simple."

There was something strange in his voice besides his cruelty. It was as if he were excited over an unexpected discovery. "What do you mean, become *like you?* I can never be like you. You are different from anybody else."

"My difference is my greatness. I am the first of my kind, but I can make others like me. I can make you like me if you will consent to our blood mixing."

I didn't know what he was offering, but it frightened me, that his blood, even a little, should get inside mine. "What would your blood do to me?" I asked.

He stood tall. "You see how strong I am. I cannot be easily killed. I see things you cannot see, I hear what you cannot hear." He leaned close, his breath cold on my cheek. "Most of all I dream things you never imagined. You can be part of that dream, Sita. Or you can begin to rot tonight, in the ground, beside your husband and child."

I did not doubt his words. His uniqueness had been obvious to me from the start. That he could transfer his qualities into another did not surprise me.

"If your blood entered into me, would I also become cruel like you?" I asked.

My question amused him. "I believe in time you would become worse than I." He leaned closer still, and I felt his teeth touch my earlobe. He took a tiny bite and sucked at the blood that flowed, and the act revolted me because of its effect on me. I liked it. I loved it even more than I loved the passion my husband gave to me in the middle of the night. I felt the true essence of Yaksha's power then, the depth of it, the space beyond the black space in the sky where the yakshinis came from. Just with that tiny bite I felt as if every drop of my blood turned from red to black. I felt invincible.

Still, I hated him, more than ever.

I took a step away.

"I watched you grow up," I said. "You watched me. You know I always speak my mind. How can I be your wife if I hate you so? Why would you want a wife like me?"

He spoke seriously. "I have wanted you for years now."

I turned my back on him. "If you want me so, it must mean you care about me. And if you care about me, then leave this place. Go away and don't come back. I am happy with my life."

I felt his cold hand on my shoulder. "I will not leave you."

"Then kill me. But leave my husband and child alone."

His grip on my shoulder tightened. Truly, I realized, he was as strong as ten men, if not more. If I cried out, Rama would be dead in a moment. Pain radiated from my shoulder into the rest of my body, and I was forced to stoop.

"No," he said. "You must come with me. It was destiny that you were there that night. It is your destiny to follow me now, to the edge of night."

"The edge of night?"

He pulled me up and kissed me hard on the lips. Once more I tasted his blood, mixed with mine. "We will live for eternity," he swore. "Just say yes. You must say yes." He paused and glanced at my house. He did not have to say it again; I understood his meaning. I was beaten.

"Yes."

He hugged me. "Do you love me?"

"Yes."

"You lie, but it doesn't matter. You will love me. You will love me forever."

He picked me up and carried me away. Into the dark forest, to a place of calm, of silence, where he opened his veins and mine with his nails, and pressed our arms together, and held them such, for what seemed forever. In that night all time was lost, and all love was tainted. He spoke to me as he changed me, but it was with words I did not understand, the sounds yakshinis must make when they mate in their black hells. He kissed me and stroked my hair.

Eventually, the power of his transfusion overwhelmed my body. My breathing, my heartbeat— they raced faster and faster, until soon they chased each other, until I began to scream, like one dropped into a boiling pot of oil. Yet, this I did not understand, and still do not. The worst of the agony was that I could not get enough of it. That it thrilled me more than the love any mortal could give to me. In that moment Yaksha became my lord, and I cried for him instead of for Vishnu. Even as the race of my breathing and heartbeat collided and stopped. Yes, as I died I forgot my God. I chose the path my father had rejected. Yes, it is the truth, I cursed my own soul by my own choice as I screamed in wicked pleasure and embraced the son of the devil.

4 ~~~

The expression "the impatience of youth" is silly.
The longer I live, the more impatient I become. True,
if nothing much is happening, I can sit perfectly still
and be content. Once I stayed in a cave for six months
and had only the blood of a family of bats to dine on.
But as the centuries have gone by, I want what I want
immediately. I enter into relationships swiftly. Therefore, in my mind, I already consider Ray and Seymour
friends, although we have just met.

Of course, I often end friendships as quickly.

It is Ray's knocking at my door that brings me out
of my rest. How does a vampire sleep? The answer is
simple. Like something dead. True, I often dream
when I sleep, but they are usually dreams of blood and

60

pain. Yet the dream I just had, of Amba and Rama and Yaksha, of the beginning, is the one I find the most painful. The pain never lessens as the time goes by. It is with a heavy step that I walk from the bedroom to answer the front door.

Ray has changed out of his school clothes into jeans and a gray sweatshirt. It is ten o'clock. A glance at Ray tells me that he is wondering what he is doing at my house after dark. This girl he has just met. This girl that has such hypnotic eyes. If he wasn't thinking about sex before, he might be thinking about it soon.

"Am I too late?" he asks.

I smile. "I'm a vampire. I stay up all night." I step aside and gesture. "Please come in, and please forgive the bare rooms. As I said, a lot of the furniture is still in the garage. The moving people couldn't get into the house when they came."

Ray glances around and nods his approval. "You said your parents are away?"

"I did say that, yes."

"Where are they?"

"Colorado."

"Where did you live in Colorado?"

"In the mountains," I say. "Would you like something to drink?"

"Sure. What do you have?"

"Water."

He laughs. "Sounds perfect. As long as you'll join me."

"Gladly. I might have a bottle of wine as well. Do you drink?"

"I have a beer every now and then."

We head for the kitchen. "Wine is much better, red wine. Do you eat meat?"

"I'm not a vegetarian, if that's what you mean. Why do you ask?"

"Just wondering," I say. He is so darling, it is hard to resist nibbling on him.

We have a glass of wine together, standing in the kitchen. We drink to world peace. Ray is anxious to get to work, he says. He is just anxious. Alone with a mortal, my aura of difference is greater. Ray knows he is with a unique female, and he is intrigued, and confused. I ask how Pat is. May as well confront his confusion.

"Fine," he says.

"Did you tell her you were coming to visit me?"

He lowers his head. He feels a twinge of guilt, but no more. "I told her I was tired and wanted to go to bed."

"You can sleep here if you want. Once you bring in the beds."

My boldness startles him. "My father would wonder where I was."

"I have a phone. You can call him." I add, "What does your father do?"

"He's a private detective."

"Sounds glamorous. Do you want to call him?"

Ray catches my eye. I catch his in return. He doesn't

62

flinch as his father did under my scrutiny. Ray is strong inside.

"Let's see how it goes and how late it gets," Ray says carefully.

He sets to work. Soon he is huffing and puffing. I help him, but only a little. Nevertheless, he comments on my strength. I tell him how I befriended Seymour and he is interested. Apparently Seymour is a friend of his as well.

"He's probably the smartest guy in the school," Rays says, lugging in a couple of dining room chairs. "He's only sixteen years old and he'll be graduating in June."

"He told me he likes to write," I say.

"He's an incredible writer. He let Pat read a couple of his short stories, and she gave them to me. They were real dark, but beautiful. One was about what goes on in the space between moments of time. It was called 'The Second Hand.' He had this character who suddenly begins to live between the moments, and finds that there is more going on there than in normal time."

"Sounds interesting. What made the story dark?"

"The guy was in the last hour of his life. But it took him a year to live it."

"Did the guy know it was his last hour?"

Ray hesitates. He must know Seymour is not well. "I don't know, Lara."

He has not used my name before. "Call me Sita," I say, surprising myself.

63

He raises an eyebrow. "A nickname?"

"Sort of. My father used to call me that."

Ray is alert to my change of tone, for I have allowed sadness to enter my voice. Or maybe it is the sound of longing, which is different from sorrow. No one I have cared about has used my real name in thousands of years. I think how nice it will be to have Ray say it.

"How long will your family be in Colorado?" Ray asks.

"I lied. My father's not there. He's dead."

"I'm sorry."

"I was thinking about him before you came." I sigh. "He died a long time ago."

"How did he die?"

"He was murdered."

Ray makes a face. "That must have been terrible for you. I know if anything ever happened to my father, I would be devastated. My mother left us when I was five."

I swallow thickly. By the strength of my reaction, I realize how involved I have allowed myself to become with the boy. All because he has Rama's eyes? There is more to it than that. He also has Rama's voice. No, not his accent surely—the average person would have said, had they heard them together, that they sounded nothing alike. But to me, with my vampire ears, the subtle aspects of their voices are almost identical. The silence between their syllables. It was Rama's deep silence that initially attracted me to him.

"You must be very close" is all I can say. But I know

I will have to bring up the father again soon. I want in that office tonight. I just hope I mopped up every drop of blood. I have no wish to be with Ray when he learns the truth.

If he ever does.

I let him finish bringing in the furniture, which takes him a couple of hours, although it took me less than twenty minutes to put it in the garage. It is after midnight. I offer him another glass of wine—a large glass—and he drinks it down quick. He is thirsty, as I am thirsty. I want his blood, I want his body. Blood drinking and sex are not that separate in my mind. Yet I am no black widow. I do not mate and kill. But the urges, the lusts—they sometimes come together. But I don't want to hurt this young man, I don't want any harm to befall him. Yet just by being with me his chances of dying are much greater. I have only to think of my history, and of the person who stalks me now. I watch as Ray sets down his empty glass.

"I should get home," he says.

"You can't drive."

"Why not?"

"You're drunk."

"I'm not drunk."

I smile. "I gave you enough alcohol to make you drunk. Face it, boy, you're trapped here for a while. But if you want to sober up quick, then take a hot tub with me. You can sweat the alcohol out of your system."

"I didn't bring my suit."

65

"I don't own a suit," I say.

He is interested—very—but doubtful. "I don't know."

I step over and rest my palms on his sweaty chest. His muscles are well developed. It would be fun to wrestle with him, I think, especially since I know who would win. I look up into his eyes; he is almost a head taller than I. He looks down at me, and he feels as if he is falling into my eyes, into bottomless wells of blue, twin skies behind which the eternal black of space hides. The realm of the yakshinis. He senses my darkness in this moment. I sense other things about him and feel a chill. So much like Rama, this boy. He haunts me. Could it be true? Those words of Krishna's that Radha had told me about love?

"Time cannot destroy it. I am that love—time cannot touch me. Time but changes the form. Somewhere in some time it will return. When you least expect it, the face of a loved one reappears. Look beyond the face and—"

Odd, but I cannot remember the last part of it. I of the perfect memory.

"I will not tell Pat," I say. "She will never know."

He draws in a breath. "I don't like lying to her."

"People always lie to one another. It's the way of the world. Accept it. It doesn't mean you have to hurt with your lies." I take his hands; they tremble slightly, but his eyes remained fastened on mine. I kiss his fingers and rub them on my cheek. "What happens with me will not hurt her."

He smiles faintly. "Is that a lie to save me hurt?"

"Maybe."

"Who are you?"

"Sita."

"Who is Sita?"

"I told you already, but you weren't listening. It doesn't matter. Come, we'll sit in the water together and I'll rub your tired muscles. You'll love it. I have strong hands."

Not long after, we are naked in the Jacuzzi together. I have had many lovers, of course, both male and female—thousands actually—but the allure of the flesh has yet to fade in me. I am excited as Ray sits with his bare back to me, my knees lightly hugging his rib cage, my hands kneading deep into the tissue along his spine. It has been a long time since I have massaged anybody and I enjoy it. The water is very hot. Steam swirls around us and Ray's skin reddens. But he says he likes it this way, so hot he feels he's being boiled alive. I, of course, don't mind boiling water. I lean over and bite him gently on the shoulder.

"Careful," he says. He does not want me to leave any marks for Pat to find.

"It will be gone in the morning." I suck a few drops of blood from his wound. Such a pleasant way to spend a night. The blood flows like an elixir down my throat, making me want more. But I resist the urge. I pinch the tip of my tongue with my teeth and a drop of blood oozes onto the small bite. It vanishes instantly. I return to my massage. "Ray?" I say.

He moans with pleasure. "Yes."

"You can make love to me if you want."

He moans some more. "You are an amazing girl, Sita."

I turn him around, slowly, easily, pleasurably. He tries not to look at my body and fails. I lean over and kiss him hard on the lips. I feel what he feels. His initial surprise—kissing a vampire is not like kissing a mortal. Many men and women have swooned just from the brush of my lips. Such is the pleasure I can give. Yet there is the painful side—my kiss often sucks the breath from a person, even when I don't intend it to. Inside, I feel Ray's heart begin to pound. I release him before there is any danger. The later it gets, the more I vow not to harm him, and the more inevitable it seems. He hugs me, all slippery and wet, and tries to catch his breath while resting his chin on my shoulder.

"Are you choking on something?" I ask.

"Yes." He coughs. "I think it's you."

I chuckle as I continue to stroke his back. "You could do worse."

"You are not like any girl I've ever met."

"You don't want just any girl, Ray."

He sits back, my naked legs still around him. He is not afraid to look me in the eyes. "I don't want to cheat on Pat."

"Tell me what you do want."

"I want to spend the night with you."

"A paradox. Which one of us is going to win?" I pause, add, "I am a master at keeping secrets. We can both win."

"What do you want from me?"

His question startles me, it is so perceptive. "Nothing," I lie.

"I think you want something."

I smile. "There is your body."

He has to smile, I sound so cute, I know. But he is not dissuaded. "What else do you want?"

"I'm lonely."

"You don't look lonely."

"I'm not when I'm looking at you."

"You hardly know me."

"You hardly know me. Why do you want to spend the night with me?"

"There is your body." But he loses his smile and lowers his head. "There is something else, too. When you look at me I feel—I feel you are seeing something nobody else sees. You have such amazing eyes."

I pull him back toward me. I kiss him. "That's true." I kiss him again. "I see right through you." Again, another kiss. "I see what makes you tick." A fourth time, a hard kiss. He gasps as I release him.

"What is that?" he asks, sucking in a breath.

"You love Pat, but you crave mystery. Mystery can be as strong as love, don't you think? You find me mysterious and you're afraid if you let me slip away you'll regret it later."

He is impressed. "That is how I feel. How did you know?"

I laugh. "That is part of the mystery."

He laughs with me. "I like you, Sita," he says.

I stop laughing. His remark—so simple, so innocent—pierces me like a dagger. No one in many years has said something as charming as "I like you" to me. The sentiment is childish, I know, but it is there nevertheless. I reach to kiss him again, knowing this time I am going to squeeze him so tight he will not be able to resist making love to me. But something makes me stop.

"Look beyond the face and you will see me."

Krishna's words to Radha that she has given to me. There is something in Ray's eyes, a light behind them, that makes me reluctant to soil them with my touch. I feel it then, that I am a creature of evil. Inside I swear at Krishna. Only the memory of him can make me feel this way. Otherwise, if we had never met, I would not care.

"I care about you, Ray." I turn away. "Come on, let's get out and get dressed. I want to talk to you about some things."

Ray is shocked at my sudden withdrawal, disappointed.

But I sense his relief as well.

Later we sit on the floor in the living room by the fire and finish the bottle of wine. Alcohol has little effect on me; I can drink a dozen truck drivers under the table. We talk of many things and I learn more details of Ray's life. He plans to go to Stanford the next fall and study physics and art—an odd double major he is quick to admit. The tuition at Stanford worries him; he doesn't know if his father can afford it. He should be worried, I think. He is a fan of modern quantum mechanics and abstract art. He works after school at a supermarket. He does not talk about Pat, and I don't bring her up. But I do steer the conversation back to his father.

"It is getting late," I say. "Are you sure you don't want to call your father and tell him that you've been sitting naked in a Jacuzzi with a beautiful blond?"

"To tell you the truth, I don't think my dad's home."

"He has a girlfriend of his own?"

"No, he's been out of town the last few days, working on a case."

"What kind of case?"

"I don't know what it is, he hasn't told me. Except that it's big and he hopes to make a lot of money on it. He's been working on it for a while now." Ray adds, "But I'm getting worried about him. He often leaves for days at a time, but he's never gone so long without calling."

"Do you have an answering machine at home?"

"Yes."

"And he hasn't even left you a message?"

"No."

"How long has he been out of touch?"

"Three days. I know that doesn't sound long, but I swear, he calls me every day."

I nod sympathetically. "I would be worried if I were you. Does he have an office in town?"

"Yes. On Tudor, not far from the ocean."

"Have you been by his office?"

"I've called his secretary, but she hasn't heard from him, either."

"That is ridiculous, Ray. You should call the police and report him missing."

Ray waves his hand. "You don't know my dad. I could never do that. He would be furious. No, I'm sure he just got wrapped up in his work, and he'll call me when he gets a chance." He pauses. "I hope."

"I have an idea," I say as if it just occurred to me. "Why don't you go down to his office and check his files to see what this big case is. You'd probably be able to find out where he is."

"He wouldn't like me looking through his files."

I shrug. "It's up to you. But if it were my father, I would want to know where he was."

"His files are all on computer. I'd have to go into his whole system, and there would be a notation left that I had done so. He has it set up that way."

"Can you get into his files? I mean, do you know the password?"

He hesitates. "How did you know he has it set up that a password is required?"

There is a note of suspicion in his question, and once more I marvel at Ray's perceptive abilities. But I do not marvel long because I have waited for this very moment since I killed his father two days ago, and I have no intention of upsetting my plan.

"I didn't," I say. "But it is a common way to protect files."

He appears satisfied. "Yeah, I can get into his files. The password is a nickname he had for me when I was a kid."

I do not need to ask him what it is, which may only increase his suspicion. Instead I jump to my feet. "Come on, let's go to his office right now. You'll sleep better knowing what he's up to."

He is startled. "Right now?"

"Well, you don't want to go looking at his files when his secretary's there. Now is the perfect time. I'll come with you."

"But it's late." He yawns. "I'm tired. I was thinking I should go home. Maybe he'll be there."

"That's an idea. Check to see if he's at home first. But if he's not, and he hasn't left you a message, then you should go to the office."

"Why are you so worried about my father?"

I stop suddenly, as if his question wounds me. "Do you have to ask?" I am referring to the comment I made about my own poor dead father and feel no shame using him that way. Ray looks suitably embarrassed. He sets down his glass of wine and gets up from the floor.

"Sorry. You may be right," he says. "I'll sleep better knowing what's going on. But if you come with me, then I'll have to bring you back here."

"Maybe." I give him a quick kiss. "Or maybe I'll just fly home."

5

At Ray's house I wait in the car while he goes in to see if his father has returned, or if there is a message from him. Naturally, I am not surprised when Ray returns a couple of minutes later downcast. The cold has sobered him up, and he is worried. He climbs into the car beside me and turns the key in the ignition.

"No luck?" I ask.

"No. But I got the key to his building. We won't have to break in."

"That's a relief." While I had Ray look away, I intended just to break the lock.

We drive to the building I visited only forty-eight hours earlier. It is another cold night. Throughout the years I have gravitated toward the warmer climates, such as my native India. Why I have chosen to come to Oregon, I am not sure. I glance over at Ray and wonder if it has something to do with him. But of course I don't believe that because I don't believe in destiny, much less in miracles. I do not believe Krishna was God, or if he was God—*maybe* he was God, I simply do not know for sure—then I do not believe he knew what he was doing when he created the universe. I have such contempt for the lotus-eyed one.

Yet, after all these years, I have never been able to stop thinking about him.

Krishna. Krishna. Krishna.

Even his name haunts me.

Ray lets us into the building. Soon we are standing outside Mr. Michael Riley's office door. Ray searches for another key, finds it. We step inside. The lights are off; he could leave them off and I would still be able to find my way around. But he turns them on and heads straight into his father's office. He sits at the computer while I stand off to one side. I survey the floor. Minute drops of blood have seeped into and dried in the cracks between the tiles. They are not noticeable to mortal eyes, but the police will find them if they search. I decide, no matter what happens, that I must return and do a more thorough cleaning. Ray boots the computer and hastily enters the secret password, thinking that I do not catch it. But I do—*RAYGUN*.

"Can you check what his latest entries were?" I ask.

"That's exactly what I'm doing." He looks over at me. "You know about computers, don't you?"

"Yes." I move closer so I can see the monitor. A menu flashes on the screen. The computer is equipped with a mouse. Ray chooses something called *Pathlist*. A list of files appears on the screen. They are dated. The number of bytes they occupy on the hard disk is also listed. A rectangular outline flashes around the file at the top.

ALISA PERNE.

Ray points to the screen. "He must be working with this person. Or else investigating her." He reaches for the Enter button. "Let's see who this woman is."

"Wait." I put my hand on his shoulder. "Did you hear that?"

"Hear what?"

"That sound."

"I don't hear anything."

"I have sensitive hearing. I heard someone outside the building."

Ray pauses and listens. "It could have been an animal."

"There it is again. Didn't you hear it?"

"No."

I appear mildly anxious. "Ray. Could you please see if anyone's there?"

He thinks a moment. "Sure. No problem. Stay here. Lock the door. I'll call to you when I return." He goes to get up.

But he exits the files before he leaves, although he leaves the computer running.

Interesting, I think. He was willing to sleep with me, but he doesn't trust me alone with his father's files. Smart boy.

The moment he's out the door, I lock it and hurry to the computer. I enter the password and call up the files. I can speed read like no mortal and have a photographic memory, yet I cannot read nearly as fast as a modern computer can copy. From the other night I know Mr. Riley has a box of formatted three-and-a-half-inch high-density diskettes in his desk. I remove two from the drawer and slip one into the computer. I am familiar with the word processor. I set it to copying the file. Mr. Riley had accumulated a lot of information on me. The Alisa Perne file is large. I estimate, given the equipment I am using, that it will take me five minutes to copy the file onto both diskettes. Ray will return before then. While the file copies, I return to the office entrance and study the lock. I can hear Ray walking down the stairs. He hums as he walks. He doesn't think there is anyone outside.

I decide to jam the lock. Taking two paper clips from Riley's desk, and bending them into usable shapes, I slip them into the tumblers. The first diskette finally fills as Ray returns from his quick outside inspection. I slip in the second diskette.

"Sita," Ray calls. "It's me. There was no one there."

I speak from the back office. "You want me to open the door for you? I locked it like you said."

"Never mind, I have the key." He inserts the key into the lock. But the door does not open. "Sita, it won't open. Have you thrown the latch?"

I approach the door slowly so that my voice will sound closer, but I have turned the monitor around so that I can keep an eye on it. The bytes accumulate quickly, but so, I suppose, do Ray's suspicions.

"There is no latch," I say. "Try the key again."

He tries a few times. "Open the door for me."

I give the appearance of trying real hard to open it. "It's stuck."

"It opened a few minutes ago."

"Ray, I'm telling you it's stuck."

"Is the lock latch turned up?"

"Yes."

"Turn it sideways."

"I can't get it to turn. Am I going to be stuck in here all night?"

"No. There's got to be a simple solution to this." He thinks a moment. "Look in my father's desk. See if you can find a pair of pliers."

I am happy to return to the desk. In a minute I have to remove my second diskette and exit the files. I open and close the drawers while I wait for the copying to finish. When it is complete, I jump into the file, scan the first page, then highlight the remainder of the file—which is several hundred pages long—and delete it. Now the Alisa Perne file contains only the first page, which holds nothing of vital importance. I return to the screen that requests the password. I put both diskettes in my back pocket. Striding back to the door, I pull out the paper clips and slip them in my back pocket as well. I open the door for Ray.

"What happened?" he asks.

"It just came unstuck."

"That's weird."

"Are you sure there's no one outside?"

"I didn't see anyone."

I yawn. "I'm getting tired."

"You were full of energy a few minutes ago. You want me to take you home now? I can come back later and study the file."

"You may as well look at it while you're here."

Ray returns to the computer. I lounge around the reception area. Ray lets out a sound of surprise. I peek in the door at him.

"What is it?" I ask.

"There isn't much in this file."

"Does it say who Alisa Perne is?"

"Not really. It just gives some background information on who contacted my dad to investigate her."

"That should be helpful."

"It's not, because even that information is cut off in midsentence." Ray frowns. "This is an odd file for my dad to create. I wonder if it's been tampered with. I could have sworn . . ." He looks at me.

"What?" I ask.

He glances back at the screen. "Nothing."

"No, Ray, tell me. You could have sworn what?" I worry he may have registered how big the file was when he first started on the computer. Certainly it is much smaller now. Ray shakes his head.

"I don't know," he says. "I'm tired, too. I'm going to look at this stuff tomorrow." He exits the files and turns off the computer. "Let's get out of here."

"OK."

Half an hour later I am at home, my real home, the mansion on the hill overlooking the ocean. I have come with the diskettes because I need my computer. My good night kiss to Ray was brief. His emotions were difficult for me to read. He is clearly suspicious of me, but that is not his dominant feeling. There is something in him that feels like a mixture of fear and attachment and gladness—very strange. But he is worried about his father, more than he was before we went to the office.

I have a variety of word processors and have no trouble loading the Alisa Perne file and bringing it up on the screen. A glance at the information shows me that Mr. Riley investigated me for approximately three months before calling me into his office. The data he dug up on me is interspersed with personal notes and comments on his correspondence with someone named "Mr. Slim." There is a fax number for Slim, but no phone number. The number indicates an office in Switzerland. I memorize it and then proceed through the file more carefully. Riley's initial contact note is interesting. Nowhere in the file are copies of Mr. Slim's faxes, just comments on them.

Aug. 8th

This morning I received a fax from a gentleman named Mr. Slim. He introduces himself as an attorney for a variety of wealthy European clients. He wants me to investigate a young woman named Alisa Perne, who lives here in Mayfair. He has little information on the woman—I have the impression that she is but one of many people he or his group is investigating. He also mentioned a couple of other women that he might have me look into in this part of the country, but he did not give me their names. He is particularly interested in Miss Perne's financial situation, her family situation, and also—and this is surprising—whether anyone she has been associated with has died violently recently. When I faxed back and asked if this woman was dangerous, he indicated that she was far more dangerous than she appeared, and that I was not to contact her directly under any circumstances. He said she appears to be only eighteen to twenty years of age.

I am intrigued, especially since Mr. Slim has agreed to deposit ten thousand dollars in my account to start me on my investigation. I have already faxed back that I will take the case. I have the young woman's address and Social Security number. I do not have a picture but intend to take one for my records, even though I have been warned to keep my distance. How dangerous can she be, at that age?

There followed an account of Riley's preliminary investigation into me. Apparently he had a contact at TRW that gave him access to information not usually available to a common investigator. I suspect Mr. Slim knew of this contact and hired Riley for that reason. Almost immediately Riley discovered that I was rich, and that apparently I had no family. The more he found out, the more eager he was to pursue the investigation, and the less information he faxed back to Mr. Slim. At one point Riley made what to him was a major decision, to use a contact on the New York Stock Exchange. By going to the man he was using up a valuable favor. But I suppose he thought I was worth it.

Sept. 21st

Miss Perne has gone to extremes to hide her financial holdings, and not just from the IRS. She has numerous accounts at various brokerage houses set up under different corporations, some off shore. Yet they appear to be coordinated by a single law firm in New York City—Benson and Sons. I tried to contact the firm directly, speaking as a rich investor, but they rebuffed my inquiries, making me suspect they handle Perne's account and no other. If that is true it is another example of this woman's wealth, for Benson and Sons has investments in the range of half a billion dollars.

Yet I have seen her—this girl—and she is as young as Mr. Slim says and very attractive. But her age confuses me, and I wonder if she has a mother somewhere who has the same name. Because many of her business dealings go back two decades, and they can all be traced to the name Alisa Perne. I am tempted to talk to her directly, despite Mr. Slim's warning.

Mr. Slim is not happy with me, and the feeling is mutual. He has the impression I have been withholding information from him and he's correct. But he has done the same with me. He still refuses to tell me the reason for his interest in this young lady, although I can imagine several scenarios. But his initial comment about her dangerous nature keeps coming back to me. Who is Alisa Perne? One of the richest people in the world obviously. But where did she get her wealth? By violent means? From her nonexistent family? I must, before I give up this case, ask her these questions myself.

I have been thinking that Mr. Slim has been paying me well, but that Alisa Perne may want to pay me more. I see already, though, that it would be unwise to let Mr. Slim know I have gone behind his back. There is a certain ruthless tone to his faxes. I don't think I ever want to meet the man. Yet I find myself looking forward to talking to Alisa.

Late September and he is on a first-name basis with me. But he did not contact me till November. What did he do during that time? I read farther and learned that he investigated my international dealings. He discovered I have property in Europe and Asia, and passports from France and India. This last fact was a revelation for him, as well it should have been. Because it appeared, accurately, that I had held the passports for more than thirty years. No wonder, I think, he asked me my age so quickly.

Finally, though, he found a violent act connected to my past. Five years earlier, in Los Angeles. The brutal slaying of a Mr. Samuel Barber. The man had been my gardener. I killed him, of course, because he had a bad habit of peering into my windows. He had seen things I didn't want talked about.

Oct. 25th

According to the police report, this man worked for her for three years. Then one morning he was found floating facedown in the ocean not far from the Santa Monica pier. His throat had been ripped out. The coroner—I spoke to him myself—was never able to determine the type of weapon. The last person to see him alive was Miss Perne.

I don't think she killed him. I like to think she didn't—the more I have studied her, the more I have come to admire her cunning and stealth. But perhaps this man learned things about her she didn't want known, and she had him killed. Certainly, she has the resources to hire whomever she pleases. When I meet with her I must ask her about her gardener. It will be another thing I can use as a bargaining chip. And I have decided I will see her soon. I have broken off all contact with Mr. Slim. In my last fax I told him that I was not able to verify any of my earlier claims about Miss Perne's personal wealth. I have since changed my fax number, so I do not know if Mr. Slim has tried to contact me again. I imagine he is not happy with me, but I am not going to lose any sleep over it.

How much should I ask from Miss Perne? A million sounds like a nice round number. I have no doubt she'll pay it to keep me quiet. What I could do with that much money. But in truth, I don't think I'll touch it. I'll just give it to Ray when he's old enough.

I will arm myself when I meet with her, just in case. But I am not worried.

That was his last entry. I am happy I have deleted the file in the computer. If the police had such information on me, they wouldn't leave me alone. It might not be a bad idea to burn down the entire office building, I muse. It wouldn't be hard to arrange. Yet such an act might draw Mr. Slim's attention to peaceful Mayfair. To young and pretty Alisa Perne.

Yet Mr. Riley was a fool to think Mr. Slim stopped watching him just because he changed his fax number. I am quite sure Slim observed him all the closer, and now that the detective has disappeared, Slim and company might even be in the neighborhood. Slim clearly has a lot of money at his disposal, and therefore a lot of power.

Yet I am confident in my own power, and I resent this unseen person shadowing me. I hold the Swiss fax number in my memory, and I contemplate what I would say to this fellow should I meet him face to face. I know that my message would be short because I do not think I would let him live long.

But I do not forget that Slim knows how dangerous I am.

That does not necessarily mean he knows I am a vampire, but it is worrisome.

I turn to my fax machine and press the On button.

Dear Mr. Slim,

This is Alisa Perne. I understand you have hired a certain Mr. Michael Riley to investigate me. I know you haven't heard from him in a while—I don't know what could have happened to him—so I thought I would contact you directly. I am prepared to meet with you, Mr. Slim, in person, and discuss whatever is on your mind.

Yours Truly,
Alisa

I attach my personal fax number and send the message. Then I wait.

I do not have to wait long. Ten minutes later a brief, and to the point, fax rolls out of my machine.

Dear Alisa,
 Where would you like to meet and when? I am
available tonight.

Sincerely,
Mr. Slim

Yes, I think, as I read the message, Slim and company are probably close by, the Swiss number notwithstanding. I figure the message went to Europe and was then sent back here—nearby. I type in my return message.

Dear Mr. Slim,
 Meet me at the end of Water Cove Pier in one
hour. Come alone. Agreed?

Again, ten minutes later.

Dear Alisa,
 Agreed.

6

The pier is a half hour from my house, in the town of Water Cove, twenty miles south of Mayfair. I arm myself before I leave the house: a snub-nosed forty-five in the pocket of my black leather coat; another smaller pistol in my right boot; a razor-sharp knife strapped inside my left boot. I am handy with a knife; I can hit a moving target a hundred yards away with a flick of my wrist. I do not believe Slim will come alone, knowing how dangerous I am. Yet he will have to bring a small army to contend with me.

I leave immediately. I want to arrive before Slim does. And I do. The pier is deserted as I cruise by in my black Ferrari. I park two blocks down from the pier and climb out. My hearing is alert. I can hear the bolt of a rifle being pulled back from over a mile away. Slim would have to come at least that close to try to assassinate me outright, and that is a possibility I consider. But all is calm, all is quiet. I walk briskly toward the end of the pier. I have chosen the meeting place for two reasons. Slim will only be able to approach me from one direction. Also, if he does arrive with overwhelming odds, then I should be able to escape by diving into the water. I can swim out a mile along the bottom of the ocean before having to surface. My confidence is high. And why shouldn't it be? In five thousand years I have never met my match.

Almost to the hour of our agreement to meet, a long white limousine pulls up to the entrance to the pier. A man and a woman climb out of the back. The man wears a black leather coat, a dark tie, a white shirt, smart black trousers. He is approximately forty-five and has the look of a hardened Navy Seal or CIA agent: the short crew cut, the bulging muscles, the quick shifting eyes. I see that his eyes are green even from two hundred yards away. His face is tan, deeply lined from the sun. There is at least one gun in his coat, possibly two.

The woman is ten years younger, an attractive brunette. She is dressed entirely in black. Her coat is bulky, as are her hidden guns. She has at least one fully automatic weapon on her. Her skin is creamy white, the line of her mouth set and hard. Her legs are long, her muscles toned. She may be an expert in karate or some such discipline. Her mind is easy to read. She has a nasty job to do and she is going to do it right. Her promised reward is great.

Yet it is clear the man is the leader. His smile is straight and thin lipped, more chilling than the girl's frown. This is Slim, I know.

Four blocks down the street I can hear another limousine parked, its engine idling. I cannot see the second car—it is hidden behind a building—but I am able to match the sound of the engines. The cars could hold maybe ten people each, I estimate. In all the odds might be twenty to one against me.

The man and the woman walk toward me without speaking. I consider escaping over the side of the pier. But I hesitate because I am a predator first and foremost; I hate to run. Also, my curiosity is high. Who are these characters and what do they want with me? Yet if they reach for their weapons, I will jump. I will be gone in the flick of an eye. It is clear to me that neither of these approaching creatures is anything but mortal.

The woman stops walking thirty yards from me. The man approaches to within ten yards but comes no closer. They do not reach for their weapons but they keep their hands ready. Down the street I hear three people get out of the second limousine. They spread out in three different directions. They carry weapons: I hear the metal brush their clothes. They take up positions—I am finally able to see them out of the corner of my eye—one behind a car; another next to a tree; the last crouched behind a sign. Simultaneously three people inside the limousine at the pier level high-powered rifles at me.

My hesitation has cost me already.

I stand in the sights of six sets of cross hairs.

My fear is still manageable. I figure I can take a bullet or two and still escape over the side. As long as they don't get me directly in the head or heart. Still, I do not want to run. I want to talk to Slim. He is the first to speak.

"You must be Alisa."

I nod. "Slim?"

"In the flesh."

"You agreed to come alone."

"I wanted to come alone. But my associates didn't think it would be wise."

"Your associates are all about. Why so many soldiers for one girl?"

"Your reputation precedes you, Alisa."

"What reputation is that?"

He shrugs. "That you are a resourceful young woman."

Interesting, I think. He is almost embarrassed by the precautions that have been taken to abduct me. He has been told to take them—ordered. He doesn't know that I am a vampire, and if he doesn't know, then probably no one with him knows since he is clearly in command of the operation. That gives me a huge advantage. But the person above him knows. I must meet this person, I decide.

"What do you want?" I ask.

"Just that you come with us for a little ride."

"To where?"

"To a place not far from here," he says.

That is a lie. We will drive a long distance if I get in his limousine. "Who sent you?"

"You will meet him if you come with me."

Him. "What is his name?"

"I'm afraid I'm not at liberty to discuss that at this time."

"What if I don't want to come?" I ask.

Slim sighs. "That would not be good. In fact, it would be very bad."

They will shoot me if I resist, without question. It is good to know.

"Did you know Detective Michael Riley?" I ask.

"Yes. I worked with him. I assume you met him?"

"Yes."

"How is he?"

I smile, my eyes cold. "I don't know."

"I'm sure you don't." He gestures with his hand. "Please come with us. A police car might be along at any moment. I'm sure neither of us wants to complicate matters."

"If I do come with you, do I have your word I will not be harmed?" I ask.

He keeps his face straight. "You have my word, Alisa."

Another lie. This man is a killer. I can smell the blood on him. I shift slightly on my feet. The rifles aimed at me all have telescopic sights. They move as I move. I estimate at least one of the shooters will hit me before I can get over the pier rail. I don't like being shot, although I have a few times. I have no choice but to go along, I decide, for the moment.

"Very well, Mr. Slim," I say. "I will come with you."

We walk toward the limousine, Slim on my right, the woman on my left. As we are almost at the entrance to the pier, the limousine down the street suddenly appears. Without picking up the men it deposited, it drives until it is parked behind the first limousine. Four men jump out. Their clothes are all similar—black sweatsuits. They point automatic weapons at me. My fear escalates. Their precautions are extraordinary. If they decide to open fire now, I will die. I think of Krishna, I don't know why. But he did tell me I would have his grace if I listened to him. And in my own way I have not disobeyed him. Slim turns in my direction.

"Alisa," he says. "I would like it if you would slowly reach in your coat and remove your gun and toss it on the ground."

I do as he asks.

"Thank you," Slim says. "Do you have any other weapons on you?"

"You will have to search me to find out."

"I prefer not to search you. I'm asking you if you have any other weapons, and that you surrender them now."

These are dangerous people, highly trained. I have

to go on the offensive, I think, quickly. I stare at Slim, my eyes boring into him. He tries to glance away but is unable to. I speak softly, knowing he hears my words as if they were whispered between his ears.

"You do not have to be afraid of me, Mr. Slim," I say. "It does not matter what you have been told. Your fear is unnecessary. I am nothing more than I appear."

I am planting a suggestion deep in his psyche, pushing buttons he already feels. But the woman takes a sudden step forward. She speaks. "Don't listen to her. Remember."

Slim shakes his head as if trying to clear it. He gestures to the woman. "Search her," he orders.

I stand perfectly still while the woman works her way down into my boots and discovers my remaining pistol and knife. I consider grabbing her and holding her as a hostage. But a study of the eyes of the men assembled tells me that they will kill her to get to me, and lose no sleep over the act. The woman disarms me and jumps back from me as if afraid she will catch something from me. All of them, without exception, are confused about why I have to be treated with such caution. Yet all of them are determined to follow orders. Slim removes two pairs of handcuffs from inside his coat. They are gold colored, and don't smell like steel—probably some special alloy. They are three times thicker than normal cuffs. Slim tosses them toward me and they land at my feet.

"Alisa," he says patiently. "I would like you to put

one pair of these around your wrists, the other pair around your ankles."

"Why?" Now I want to stall for time. Maybe a police officer will come by. Of course, these people would just kill the officer.

"We have a long drive ahead of us, and we want you safely tucked away before we allow you in our car," Slim says.

"You said we didn't have far to go?"

"Put on the cuffs."

"All right." I put them on, marveling once more at their preparation.

"Press them together so that they lock," Slim suggests.

I do so. They click. "Happy?" I ask. "Can we go?"

Slim removes a black eye mask from his pocket, similar to the kind people wear to bed. He steps toward me. "I want you to put this on," he says.

I hold out my cuffed hands. "You'll have to put it on me."

He takes another step toward me. "Your hands are free enough to put it on."

I catch his eye again; it may be my last chance. "You do not have to be so afraid of me, Slim. Your fear is ridiculous."

He hurries toward me and covers my eyes. I hear his voice.

"You're right, Alisa," he says.

He grabs my arm and pulls me toward the limousine.

We drive south on the Coast Highway. All is dark, but I still have my sense of direction. All my senses with the exception of my eyes are very alert. Slim sits on my right, the woman on my left. Four burly men sit across from us; two up front. I count the breaths. The second limousine follows a hundred yards behind. They picked up their three marksmen before we hit the road.

There are no incidental smells in the limousine. The car is new. There is no food in the limousine, but there is drink in the bar: sodas, juice, water. There is a faint smell of gunpowder in the air. One or more of the guns in the vehicle has recently been fired. Everybody has his gun out, in his hands or resting in his lap. Only the woman keeps hers aimed at me. She is the most afraid of me.

Several miles go by. The breathing of the people around me begins to slow, to lengthen and deepen. They are relaxing, except for the woman. They think the difficult part is over. Careful, I test the strength of the cuffs. The metal is incredibly hard. I will not be able to break it. But that doesn't mean I can't get around. I can hop, even bound, far more quickly than any mortal can run. I might be able to grab one of the automatic weapons from the lap of one of the men across from me and shoot and kill most of the people in the limousine before they can shoot me back. Then again, the woman might put a bullet in my brain first. Also, I know the car behind us is operating under strict instructions. The pattern in the abduction is clear. If they see me attacking, they will open fire without hesitation. Everyone in the first limousine will die, and I will be one of them. This is why there are two cars, not one.

I must try another way.

I let another thirty minutes go by. Then I speak.

"Slim. I have to go to the bathroom."

"I'm sorry, that's not possible," he says.

"I have to go bad. I drank an entire bottle of Coke before meeting you."

"I don't care. We are not stopping."

"I'll pee all over the seat. You'll have to sit in it."

"Pee if you must."

"I will do it."

He doesn't respond. More miles go by. Since Slim carried the cuffs, I decide he must be the one who has the key to open them. The arm of the woman beside me begins to tire. She lowers her weapon hand: I hear the rustling of her clothing. I estimate our speed to be sixty miles an hour. We are maybe fifty miles south of Water Cove. Seaside is approaching; I can hear the town up ahead; the two all night gas stations; the twenty-four-hour doughnut shop.

"Slim," I say.

"What?"

"I have a problem besides having to pee."

"What is it?"

"I'm having my period. I have to get to a rest room. I need only two minutes. You and your lady friend can come with me into the rest room. You can point your guns at me the whole time if you want, I don't care. If you do not stop, we will have a mess here and we will have it soon."

"We are not stopping."

I raise my voice. "This is ridiculous! I am bound hand and foot. You are armed left and right. I just have to go to the bathroom for two minutes. For God's sake, what kind of sick person are you? Do you like piss and blood?"

Slim considers. I hear him lean forward and glance at the woman. "What do you think?" he asks.

"We are not supposed to stop for any reason," she says.

"Yeah, but what the hell." He adds a line, and as he does so, I hear my implanted suggestion. "What harm can she do?"

"She must be guarded at all times," the woman insists.

"I already said you two can follow me into the rest room," I say.

"So we have your permission?" the woman asks sarcastically. The sound of her voice is aggravating. She is from Germany—the east side. I hope she follows me into the bathroom. I have a surprise for her. "I have no sanitary napkins," she says.

"I will use whatever is available," I say softly.

"It is up to you," the woman says to Slim.

He considers, studying me, I know. Then he decides. "Hell, call the others. Tell them we're stopping at the first gas station. We'll pull around back."

"They won't like that," the man up front says.

"Tell them they can talk to me if they are worried," Slim says. He turns toward me. "Happy?"

"Thank you," I say in my velvety voice. "I won't cause any problems. You really can accompany me if you want."

"You can be sure I will, sister," Slim says—as if it were his own idea. I want those keys.

The call is made. We slow as we enter Seaside. The driver spots a gas station. I hear the all-night attendant making change. We drive around the side, the second limousine close behind us. The car stops. Slim opens his door.

"Stay here," he says.

We wait for Slim to return. The woman has her gun pointed at my head again. She just doesn't like my looks, I suppose. But the men are relaxed. They are thinking, all this security for what? Slim comes back. I hear him unholster his weapon.

"There will be two of us on you," he says. "Don't get smart."

"You have to take this thing off my eyes," I say. "I'll make a mess if I can't see."

Of course I can reach up and remove it myself, when I make my move. But to have it removed now will save me the extra step. Also, I want my vision to plan when to attack. Finally, by asking them to take it off, I emphasize my helplessness.

"Any other requests?" Slim asks.

"No."

He reaches over and pulls off the mask. "Happy?"

I smile at him, grateful. "I will be when I get in the bathroom."

He stares at me, doubt and confusion touching his face. "Who the hell are you?"

"A girl with a bad attitude," I say.

The woman pokes her pistol at my temple. "Get out. You have two minutes. No more."

I climb out of the car. The guys in the other limousine are all out, their weapons hidden but handy. They form a wall between me and the front of the gas station. I hope none of them accompanies me into the rest room. But Slim and the woman are determined to stay with me. I give the watching gang a timid smile as I shuffle past. They chew gum. They stare at my body. They, too, wonder what all the fuss is about. The woman goes into the bathroom first. I follow, Slim on my tail. No one else comes in. The door closes behind us.

I strike immediately. I have it all planned.

In a move too fast for a mortal eye to follow, I whirl and knock Slim's pistol away. Raising my cuffed hands over my head, I bring them down on top of his skull. I use only a fraction of my strength; I want to stun him, no more. He topples to the floor as the woman turns, bringing up her gun. I kick it from her hand by lashing out with both my feet. She blinks as I land upright. She opens her mouth to say something when I grab her face with both my hands. My grip is ferocious; there is blood even before I kill her, around her eyes. My nails destroy her vision permanently.

There is lots more blood when I smash the back of her head on the tiled wall. The plaster cracks under the blow sending up a miniature cloud of white dust shot through with streaks of red. Likewise her skull cracks, in many places. She sags in my arms, the blood from her mortal wounds soaking the front of my leather jacket. She is dead; I let her drop.

The door is closed but not locked. Quickly I press it tight and lock it. At my feet Slim lets out a moan. I reach down and grab him and press him against the wall beside the stain of the dead woman's brains. My hands go around his throat. Perhaps five seconds have elapsed since we entered the bathroom. Slim winces and opens his eyes. They focus quickly when they see me.

"Slim," I say softly. "Look around you. Look at your dead partner. Her brains are leaking out of her head. She's a mess—it's terrible. I'm a terrible person. I'm also a very strong person. You can feel how strong I am, can't you? That's why your boss wanted you to be so careful with me. You can't screw with me and get away with it. Please don't even consider it. Now, let me tell you what I want. Reach in your pocket and pull out the key to these cuffs. Unlock them. Don't shout out to the others. If you do these things, then maybe I will let you go. If you don't, your brains will be all over the floor like your partner's.

Think about it for a moment, if you want, but don't think too long. You can see what an impatient person I am."

He stammers. "I don't have the keys."

I smile. "Bad answer, Slim. Now I will have to go through your pockets and find them. But I'll have to make sure you're lying perfectly still while I do so. I'm going to have to kill you."

He's scared. He can hardly talk. He accidentally steps in the mess dripping out of the woman's head. "No. Wait. Please. I have the keys. I will give you the keys."

"That's good. Good for you." I release my grip slightly. "Undo the locks. Remember, if you shout out, you die."

His hands shake badly. All his training has not prepared him for me. His eyes keep straying to what I have done to the woman's head. A crumpled accordion of bloody assault. Finally, though, Slim gets my cuffs off. My relief at being free is great. Once more, I feel my usual invincibility. I am a wolf among sheep. The slaughter will be a pleasure. I toss the cuffs in the wastebasket. Just then someone knocks at the door. I press my fingers deep into the sides of Slim's throat.

"Ask what it is," I say. I let go just enough to allow him to speak.

He coughs. "What is it?"

"Everything OK in there?" a man asks. They have heard noise.

"Yeah," I whisper.

"Yeah," Slim says.

The man outside tries the doorknob. Of course it is locked. "What's happening?" the man asks. He is the suspicious type, to be sure.

"Everything is cool," I whisper.

"Everything is cool," Slim manages. It is no wonder the guy outside doesn't believe Slim; he sounds like he's about to weep. The guy outside tries the door again.

"Open the door," he demands.

"If we go out that way," I ask Slim, "will they shoot us both?"

He croaks. "Yes."

I study the bathroom. The wall against which I hold Slim is completely tiled; it appears to be the thickest wall in the rest room. But the wall behind the lone toilet looks flimsy. I suspect on the other side of it might be the late-night attendant's office space. Keeping Slim pinned with my left hand, I reach down and pick up the dead woman's automatic weapon.

"We are going to go through that wall there," I say. "I will kick it in, then we will move. I don't want you wrestling with me. If you do, I will rip out your throat. Now tell me, what is behind this gas station? A field? Another building? A road?"

"Trees."

"Trees like in the forest?"

"Yes."

"Excellent." I drag him into the stall. "Prepare yourself for a fun ride."

Still holding on to Slim, I leap into the air several

feet and plant three swift kicks on the wall above the toilet. It splinters and I break through what is left of it with a slash of my right arm. We enter the all-night attendant's office. Before he can turn to identify us, I strike him on the back of the head. He goes down, probably still alive. I kick open the door to the outside. The fresh air is sweet after the staleness of the rest room. Behind me I hear the bathroom door being broken down. There are shocked gasps when they see what I have done to poor Miss Germany.

Dragging Slim, I come around the two parked limos from behind. There are men inside the rest room, more hovering at the door, still more getting out of the first limo. I raise the automatic weapon, an Uzi, and let loose a spray of bullets. Screams rent the air. Several of the men go down. Others reach for their guns. I empty the clip in their direction and drop the Uzi to the ground. I don't need it, I am a vampire. I need only my natural power.

In a blur, still holding on to Slim, I cross the parking lot and enter the trees. A trail of bullets chases us. One of them catching me in the butt, the right cheek. The wound burns, but I don't mind. The woods are mainly pine, some spruce. A hill rises above us, a quarter of a mile to the top. I pull Slim to the pinnacle, and then back down the other side. A stream crosses our path and we splash through it. The old belief is not true; running water does not bind my steps.

By now I have badly wrenched Slim's neck. Behind us I hear men entering the forest, six of them, spreading out, searching for us. I can hear others at the gas station, moaning in pain, the sputtering breath of still others dying. I literally pick Slim off his feet and carry him a half mile upstream, running faster than a deer in her prime, even with the bullet in me. Then I throw Slim down behind a cluster of bushes. I straddle his chest. He looks up at me with eyes wide with fear. I must be little more than a shadow in his vision. Yet I can see him perfectly. I reach around to my back side, digging my fingers into the torn tissue. I pull out the bullet and toss it aside. The wound begins to heal immediately.

"Now we can talk," I say.

"W-who?" he stutters. I lean over, my face in his.

"That is the magic question," I say. "Who sent you after me?"

He is struggling for breath, although I am no longer holding him by the throat. "You are so strong. How is it possible?"

"I am a vampire."

He coughs. "I don't understand."

"I am five thousand years old. I was born before recorded history began. I am the last of my kind . . . I believe I am the last. But the person who sent you after me knew of my great strength. You were carefully prepared. That person must know that I am a vampire. I want that person." I breathe on his face and know he feels the chill of the Grim Reaper. "Tell me who he is, where I can find him."

He is in shock. "Is this possible?"

"You have seen a demonstration of my power. Do you really want me to give you another one?"

He trembles. "If I tell you, will you let me live?"

"Perhaps."

He swallows thickly, perspiring heavily. "We work out of Switzerland. I have only met my boss a few times. His name is Graham—Rick Graham. He is very wealthy. I do odd jobs for him, my people and I. Two years ago he set us searching for someone who fit your description."

"How did he describe me?"

"The way you look. Other things as well. He said you would be rich, private, have no family. He said there would be mysterious deaths connected with your name."

"Did he know my name?"

"No."

"Has he had you look for anyone else?"

"No. Only someone who fit your description." He grimaces in pain. "Could you get off me? I think you broke several of my ribs when you pulled me through the trees."

"You were not concerned about my comfort in the car."

"I stopped to let you go to the bathroom."

"That was your mistake." My voice is cold.

He is very afraid. "What are you going to do to me?"

"What is Graham's address? Is he in Switzerland?"

"He is never in one place. He travels constantly."

"Why?"

"I don't know why. Maybe he looks for you."

"But is he on the West Coast now? In Oregon?"

"I don't know."

He is telling the truth. "But you were taking me to him tonight, weren't you?"

"I don't know. We were to drive you to San Francisco. I was to call from a certain phone booth. I can give you the number. It is in Switzerland."

"Say it." He gives me the number. I consider. "I faxed you in Switzerland earlier tonight. Yet you were here. It is possible Graham is here as well?"

"It is possible. We have relays."

"Do you have a business card, Slim?"

"What?"

"A card. Give me your card."

"My wallet is in my front right pocket."

I rip away his pocket. "So it is." I stuff the wallet in my back pocket. My pants are soaked with blood, some of my own, some of the woman's. In the distance I hear two of the men coming my way. Farther off I hear a police siren, heading south on Coast Highway. The men hear it as well. I can practically read their thoughts, they are so obvious. This woman is a monster. If she has Slim, Slim is dead. She will probably kill us if we do catch up with her. The police are coming. We'd better get the hell out of here and chalk it up to a bad night.

The men reverse their direction, back toward the

gas station. I lovingly stroke the sides of Slim's face. Of course there is no possibility I will let him live.

"Why do you work for Graham?" I ask.

"The money."

"I see. Tell me what Graham looks like?"

"He is tall, six three maybe. His hair is dark. He wears it long."

Now I am the one who trembles. "What color are his eyes?"

"Blue."

"Pale blue?"

"Yes. They are frightening."

My voice whispers. "Like mine?"

"Yes. God, please don't kill me. I can help you, miss. I really can."

Yaksha.

It is not possible, I think, after all this time. The stories, why did I listen to them? Just because they said he was dead? He probably invented them. But why does he come for me now? Or is that the most foolish question of all? These people had orders to shoot if I so much as burped. He must want me dead.

He must be afraid of what Krishna told him.

"You have helped me enough," I tell Slim.

He pants. "What are you going to do? Don't do it!"

My fingers reach down to his throat, my long nails caressing the big veins beneath his flesh. "I told you what I am. And I'm hungry. Why shouldn't I suck you dry? You are no saint. You kill without conscience. At least when someone dies in my arms, I think kind thoughts about him."

He cries. "Please! I don't want to die."

I lean over. My hair smothers him.

"Then you should never have been born," I say.

I open him up. I open my mouth.

I take my pleasure slowly.

7 ~~

The body I bury beneath the stream. It is a favorite place of mine. Police seldom look under running water. I hear them in the distance, the law, at the gas station, maybe two black and whites. They have a shoot-out with the boys in the limos. The boys win. I hear them tear away at high speed. They are clever. I believe they will get away.

Yet if I want them, I will have them later.

More police can be heard approaching. I decide to exit the forest the back way. I jog through the trees, setting cross-country records. Six miles later finds me at a closed gas station on a deserted road. There is a phone booth. I think of calling Seymour Dorsten, my archery buddy. It is a mad thought. I would do better to keep running till I find a busier road, a few parked cars. I can hot-wire any car in less than a minute. I am soaked through with blood. It would be madness to involve Seymour in this night's dirty business. He might tell his mother. Yet I want him involved. I trust the little guy. I don't know why.

Information gives me his number. I call. He answers on the second ring and sounds alert. "Seymour," I say. "This is your new friend."

"Lara." He is pleased. "What are you doing? It's four in the morning."

"I have a little problem I need your help with." I check the street sign. "I am at a gas station on Pinecone Ave. I am six miles inland from Seaside, maybe seven, due east of the city. I need you to come get me. I need you to bring a change of clothing for me: pants and a sweatshirt. You must come immediately and tell no one what you're doing. Are your parents awake?"

"No."

"What are you doing awake?"

"How did you know I was awake?"

"I'm psychic," I say.

"I was having a dream about you. I just woke up from it minutes ago."

"You can tell me about it later. Will you come?"

"Yes. I know where you're talking about. Is it a Shell station? It's the only one on that road."

"Yes. Good boy. Hurry. Don't let your parents hear you leave."

112

"Why do you need the change of clothes?"

"You'll understand when you see me."

Seymour arrives a little over an hour later. He is shocked at my appearance, as well he should be. My hair is the color of a volcano at sunset. He stops the car and jumps out.

"What happened to you?" he asks.

"A few people tried to rough me up, but I got away. I don't want to say any more than that. Where are the clothes?"

"Wow." He doesn't take his eyes off me as he reaches back into the front seat. He has brought me blue jeans and a white T-shirt and two different sweaters: one green, the other black. I will wear the black one. I begin to strip right in front of him. The boy has driven far and deserves a thrill. "Lara," he says, simply amazed.

"I am not shy." I unbutton my pants and wiggle them down. "Do you have a towel or some kind of old cloth in the car?"

"Yes. You want to wipe off some of the blood?"

"Yes. Get it for me please."

He gives me a stained dish towel. Now I am completely naked, the sweat on my skin sending off faint whiffs of steam in the cold night air. I clean my hair as best I can and wipe the blood from my breasts. Finally I reach for the clothes he has brought.

"Are you sure you don't want to call the police?" he asks.

"I am sure." I pull the T-shirt on first.

Seymour chuckles. "You must have had a bow and a few arrows with you when they caught up with you."

"I was armed." I finish dressing, putting my boots back on, and bundle my clothes together. "Wait here a second. I have to get rid of these."

I bury the clothes in the trees, but before I do so I remove my car keys and Slim's wallet from my pants pocket. I am back with Seymour in ten minutes. He is behind the wheel with the engine on, the heater up high. In his frail condition he must get cold easily. I climb in beside him.

"My car is in Seaside, not far from the pier," I say. "Can you take me there?"

"Sure." He puts the car in gear. We head north. "What made you call me?"

"Your sexy mind."

He laughs. "You knew I was the only one in town who wouldn't immediately report you to the authorities."

"I am serious about you keeping this private."

"Oh, I will."

I smile and pat his leg. "I know you will. Besides your sexy mind, I called you because I know you don't object to a little stroll on the wild side from time to time."

He eyes me through his thick glasses. "You may be a little wild even for my tastes. You can't even tell me a little something about what happened?"

"You would have trouble believing the truth."

He shakes his head. "Not after this dream I had about you. It was amazing."

"Tell me about it."

"I dreamed you were on a battlefield and a whole army of demons was approaching you from every direction. They had all kinds of weapons: axes and swords and hammers. Their faces were hideous. They were jeering loudly, anxious to rip you to shreds. Where you were standing was a bit above the rest of the field, on a grassy knoll. But the rest of the field was a reddish dust color, as if it were a plain on Mars. The sky was filled with smoke. There was only you against thousands. It looked hopeless. But you were not afraid. You were dressed like an exotic goddess. Your chest was covered with silver mail. You had a jeweled sword in your right hand, emerald earrings set in gold that chimed as you slowly surveyed the army around you. A peacock feather stood in your braided hair, and you wore tall boots made of fresh hide. They dripped with blood. You smiled as the front rank of the demons went to strike you. You raised your sword. Then you stuck out your tongue."

"My tongue?"

"Yeah. This was the scary part. Your tongue was real long. It was purple, bloody—it looked as if you had taken a bite or two out of it. When you stuck it out, all the demons froze and acted afraid. Then you made this sound at the back of your throat. It's hard to describe. It was a loud sound, nasal. It echoed across the whole battlefield, and as it reached the ear of each demon, he toppled over dead."

"Wow," I say. The part about the tongue naturally reminds me of the yakshini. There is now no question in my mind. Seymour is supernaturally sensitive to emotional states. More than that he seems to have linked up with me somehow, formed an intuitive bond with me. Certainly, I have with him. I am mystified. I cannot logically understand my great affection for him. It is not the same as my love for Ray, my passion for the son of Riley. For me, Seymour is like a younger brother, a son even. In five thousand years I have never had a child except for Lalita. I would like to play with this young man. "Is there more?" I ask.

"Yes," he says. "But you might not want to hear this part. It's pretty gross."

"I do not gross out easily."

"After seeing you tonight, I imagine you don't. When all the demons were dead, you began to stride about the battlefield. Sometimes you would step on a demon's head and it would be crushed and the brains inside would ooze out. Sometimes you would stop and cut off the head of a demon. You accumulated a number of heads. You were making a necklace out of them. Other times you would find a demon that wasn't entirely dead. These you would grab by the throat and raise up to your mouth." He pauses for effect. "You would open their necks with your nails and drink their blood."

"Doesn't sound so bad." He continues to amaze me. His dream is like a metaphor for the entire night. "Anything else?"

"One last thing. When you were through walking about, and stood still, the flesh of the demons began to decay. In seconds they were nothing but dust and crumbling bones. Then the sky began to darken more. There was something in the sky, some kind of huge bird, circling above you. It disturbed you. You raised your sword to it and let out that weird sound again. But the bird kept circling, getting lower and lower. You were afraid of it. It did not seem you could stop it."

"That hasn't happened yet," I whisper.

"Pardon?"

"Nothing. What kind of bird was it?"

"I can't be sure."

"Was it a vulture?"

"Maybe." He frowns. "Yeah, I think it was." He gives me an uneasy look. "You don't like vultures?"

"They are symbolic of a forsaken ending."

"I didn't know that. Who told you that?"

"Experience." I sit silent with my eyes closed for a few minutes. Seymour knows not to disturb me. The boy saw the present, I think, why couldn't he see the future? Yaksha is circling me, closer and closer. My old tricks will stop him. My strength, my speed, were never a match for his. The night is almost over. The day will soon be. But for us the day is the night, the time to rest, to hide, to despair. I know in my heart that Yaksha is not far.

Yet Krishna said I would have his grace if I obeyed him.

And I have. But what did he promise Yaksha? The same?

I do not believe so.

The scriptures say the Lord is mischievous.

I think Krishna told him the opposite.

I open my eyes. I stare at the road in front. "Are you afraid of dying, Seymour?"

He speaks carefully. "Why do you ask?"

"You have AIDS. You know it."

He sucks in a breath. "How did you know?"

I shrug. "I know things. You know things as well. How did you catch it? You don't seem gay. You were staring at me too hard when I was naked."

"You have an awesome body."

"Thank you."

He nods. "I am HIV positive. I suppose I have full-blown AIDS. I have the symptoms: fatigue; skin cancer; bouts of parasitic pneumonia. But I've been feeling good the last few weeks. Do I look that bad?"

"You look awesome. But sick."

He shakes his head. "I was in a car crash five years ago. Ruptured my spleen. I was with an uncle. He died, but I got to the hospital in time. They operated on me and gave me two pints of blood. It was after the test for HIV was routine with all donated blood, but I guess this batch slipped through the cracks." He shrugs. "So I'm another statistic. Is that why you asked about fear of dying?"

"It was one reason."

"I am afraid. I think anybody would be lying if he said he wasn't afraid of death. But I try not to think about it. I'm alive now. There are things I want to do . . ."

"Stories you want to write," I interrupt.

"Yes."

I reach over and touch his arm. "Would you write a story about me someday?"

"What should I write?"

"Whatever comes to mind. Don't think about it too much. Just whatever is there, write it down."

He smiles. "Will you read it if I write it?"

I take my hand back and relax into the seat. My eyes close again; I feel suddenly weary. I am not mortal, at least I didn't think I was until tonight. Yet now I feel vulnerable. I am as afraid of death as everyone else.

"If I get the chance," I say.

8

Seymour takes me to my car and tries to follow me back to Mayfair. But I speed away at a hundred miles an hour. He is not insulted, I'm sure. I warned him I'm in a hurry.

I go to my mansion by the sea. I have not described it before because to me a house is a house. I do not fall in love with them as do some mortals. The house is on twenty acres of property, at the top of a wooded yard that reaches from my front porch all the way down to the rocky shore. The driveway is narrow and winding, mostly hidden. The house itself is mainly brick, Tudor style, unusual for this part of the country. There are three stories; the top one has a wide view of the sea and coast. There are many rooms, fireplaces and such, but I do most of my living in the living room, even though it has wide skylights that I have yet to board up. I do not need a lot of space to be happy, although I have lived in mansions or castles since the Middle Ages. I could be quite happy living in a box. I say that as a joke.

My tastes in furniture are varied. At present I surround myself with lots of wood: the chairs, the tables, the cabinets. I sleep on a bed, not in a coffin, a grand mahogany affair with a black lace canopy. I have gathered art over the centuries and have a vast and expensive collection of paintings and sculptures in Europe, but none of it in America. I have gone through phases where art is important to me, but I am not in one now. Still, I have a piano wherever I go. I play almost every day, and with my speed and agility, I am the most accomplished pianist in the world. But I seldom write music, not because I am not creative, but because my melodies and songs are invariably sad. I do not know why—I do not think of myself as a sad vampire.

Tonight, though, I am an anxious vampire, and it has been centuries since I felt the emotion. I do not like it. I hurry into my home and change and then rush back out to my car. My concern is for Ray. If it is Yaksha after me, and I have little doubt now, then he may try to get to me through Ray. It seems a logical course to me based on the fact that Yaksha probably first became aware of me through Ray's father. I now suspect Yaksha has been observing me since I first visited Mr. Riley's office. But why he didn't attack immediately, I don't know. Maybe he wanted to study the enemy he hadn't seen for so long, to probe for weaknesses. Yet Yaksha, more than any living or nonliving being, already knows where I am vulnerable.

I am still in shock that he is alive.

I drive to Ray's house and leap to the front door. I half expect to find him gone, abducted. For a moment I consider not ringing the doorbell, but to just barge in. I have to remind myself that Ray is not Seymour, capable of accepting anything that comes along. I knock on the door.

Pat surprises me when she answers.

The girlfriend is not happy to see me.

"What are you doing here?" Pat demands.

"I have come to see Ray." Pat must have called Ray's house while he was at my place, probably several times. She must have called not long after he came home. He probably invited her over to pacify her concerns. But she does not look that pacified.

"He's asleep," Pat says. She starts to slam the door in my face. I stick out my arm. She tries to force it shut. Naturally, she is not successful. "Get out of here. Can't you tell when you're not wanted?"

"Pat," I say patiently. "Things are not as they appear. They are much more complicated. I need to see Ray because I believe he is in danger."

"What are you talking about?"

"I cannot tell you, not easily. I have to talk to Ray

and I have to talk to him now." I put my eye on her. "Please do not try to stop me. It would not be a good idea."

She cowers under my stare. I move to press her farther, but it becomes unnecessary. Upstairs, I hear Ray climb out of bed. I wait a few seconds, then call out his name.

"Ray!" I say. I hear his steps quicken. We both do.

"He's mine," Pat mutters as we wait for Ray to arrive. She is sad, seemingly defeated already. Instinctively she knows I have a power she does not, beyond my beauty. Her love for him is genuine, I can see that, a rare thing in a girl her age.

"Have hope," I say sincerely.

Ray appears. He has on sweat pants, no top. "What's going on?" he asks.

"Lots of things. I need to talk to you, alone." I glance at Pat. "If that would be all right?"

Her eyes are damp. She lowers her head. "I can just go," she mumbled.

Ray puts a hand on her shoulder. "No." He gives me a sharp glance. I have to be careful. "Tell me what it is?"

"It has to do with your father," I say.

He is concerned. "What is it?"

I am stubborn. "I must tell you alone." I add, "I'm sorry, Pat."

Ray rubs her back. "Go upstairs to bed. I'll be up in a few minutes."

Pat shakes her head, giving me a look as she leaves. "I don't think so."

When we are alone, Ray wants me to explain myself. "You told me you wouldn't hurt Pat," he says.

"My coming here could not be helped. I have not been entirely honest with you, Ray. I think you suspect that."

"Yes. You tampered with the file on my father's computer."

"How did you know?"

"When I turned on the computer, I noted the size of the file. It was large. When I returned, most of it had been deleted."

I nod. "That file was about me. Your father was investigating me. He was hired by some people to do so, one man in particular. This man is dangerous. Tonight he sent some people to abduct me. I managed to get away. I believe he may come after you next."

"Why me?"

"Because he knows you are my friend. I believe he has been watching me today and tonight. Also, even though this man hired your father, your father did not part company with him on the best of terms."

"How do you know that?"

"The people who came for me tonight told me."

"What do you mean, they came for you? Were they armed?"

"Yes."

"Then how did you get away from them?"

"They made a mistake, and I am resourceful. I do

not want to get into all of that now. What is important is that you come with me now."

"I'm not going anywhere until you tell me where my father is."

"I can't."

"You don't know?"

I hesitate. It is not easy for me to lie to those I love. "No."

Ray is suspicious. His sense of the truth, and therefore of lies, is remarkable. "Do you think my father is in danger?" he asks.

"Yes."

He hears the truth in that word. "We should call the police."

"No!" I grab his arm. "The police cannot help us. You have to come with me. Trust me, Ray. I can tell you more once we are at my house."

"What will we do at your house that we can't do here?"

"You will see," I say.

Ray consents to accompany me. He goes upstairs to say goodbye to Pat. I hear her crying, and wonder if she will not shed a stream of tears in the days to come. I could be wrong. I could be bringing Ray into danger, not away from it. I scan up and down the street but see nothing. Yet I feel eyes on me, powerful eyes such as my own. I wonder if I am not reaching for Ray because I am afraid.

Maybe afraid to die alone.

Ray reappears in a few minutes, dressed. We go to

my car. He has not seen it before and marvels that I have a Ferrari. We drive toward my mansion and he wonders why we are not going the same way as before. I tell him I have two houses.

"I am very rich," I say.

"Is that one of the reasons my father was investigating you?" he asks.

"Yes. Indirectly."

"Have you spoken to my father?"

"Yes."

"When?"

"Two and a half days ago."

"Where?"

"At his office."

Ray is annoyed. "You didn't tell me. Why did you speak to him?"

"He called me into his office."

"Why?"

I have to be more careful than ever. "He wanted to tell me that I was being investigated."

"He wanted to warn you?"

"I believe so. But—"

"What?"

"He didn't fully understand who had hired him, the nature of the man."

"But you know this man?"

"Yes. From a long time ago."

"What's his name?"

"He changes his name often."

"Like you?" Ray asks.

126

The boy is full of surprises. I reach over and touch his leg. "You are worried about your father. I understand. Please try not to judge me too harshly."

"You are not being completely honest with me."

"I'm telling you what I can."

"When you say my father is in danger, what exactly do you mean? Would this man kill my father?"

"He has killed in the past."

The space inside the car is suddenly cramped. Ray hears beyond my words. "Is my father dead already?" he asks quietly.

I have to lie, I have no choice. "I don't know."

We arrive at my house. No one has come while I was away, I can tell. I activate the security system. It is the most elaborate available on the market. Every wire of every section of fence around my house is now heavily electrified. There are motion sensors and laser beams and radar tracking the perimeter. I know it will not stop Yaksha for a second if he wishes to come for me. At a minimum he has twice my strength and speed. In reality I think he is much more powerful than that.

Ray wanders around my house, taking in the sights. He pauses and looks out over the ocean. A waning moon, half full, hangs over the dark shadow of the water. We face west, but behind us, in the east, I detect a hint of dawn.

"What next?" he asks.

"What do you want to do next?"

He faces me. "You are waiting for this man to come here."

"Perhaps. He could come."

"You said something about arming yourself. Do you have guns here?"

"Yes. But I'm not going to give you one. It would not help."

"Are you some kind of expert with guns?"

"Yes."

He is exasperated. "Who the hell are you, Sita? If that is even your real name."

"It is my real name. Few people know it. It is the name my father gave me. The man I am talking about—he is the one who murdered my father."

"Why don't we call the police?"

"This man is very powerful. He has almost unlimited resources. The police would not be able to stop him if he wants to hurt us."

"Then how are you going to stop him?"

"I don't know if I can."

"Then why are we here? Why don't we just get in the car and drive away?"

His question is an interesting one; it has a certain logic to it. I have considered the option since disposing of Slim. Yet I do not believe that I can run successfully from Yaksha, not once he has got me in his sights, which he obviously does. I do not like to postpone the inevitable.

"You can drive away if you want," I say. "You can take my car and go home. Or you can take my car and drive to Los Angeles. That might be the best thing for you to do. I can tell you for a fact that while you are here you are in extreme danger."

"Then why did you bring me here?"

I turn away. "I do not know why. But I think—I don't know."

"What?"

"This man—his real name is Yaksha—he knows you are my friend. You are part of the equation that deals with me—in his mind."

"What do you mean?"

I turn back to Ray. "He has been watching me since I saw your father, I'm sure of it. But he has not come for me personally. Oh, he sent his people after me, but that is not the same thing, not to him and not to me."

"You think that I afford you some protection?"

"Not exactly. More, I think he is curious about my relationship with you."

"Why?"

"I do not make friends easily. He knows that much."

Ray sighs. "I don't even know if I am your friend."

His words sting, more than the bullet I was hit with earlier in the night. I reach out and touch his face. Such a beautiful face, so like Rama's, even though they do not look that much alike. Their essence is similar. Maybe Krishna was right. Maybe their souls are the same, if there are such things. I doubt I have one.

"I care more for you than I have cared for anyone in

129

a long time," I say. "I am much older than I look. I have been more lonely than I have been willing to admit to myself. But when I met you, that loneliness eased. I am your friend, Ray, even if you do not want to be mine."

He stares at me, as if he, too, knows me, then lowers his lips to kiss my hand that touches him. His next words come to me as if from far away.

"Sometimes I look at you and you do not look human."

"Yes."

"You're like something carved from glass."

"Yes."

"Old but always new."

"Yes."

"You said you are a vampire."

"Yes."

But he does not ask me if I am a vampire. He knows better. He knows I will tell him the truth, and he does not want to hear it. He kisses my hand again, and I lean forward to kiss his lips. Long and deep—he does not smother this time and I am glad. He wants to make love, I can tell, and I am very glad.

I start a roaring blaze in the living room fireplace, many logs piled high. There is a rug from ancient Persia on top of the wall-to-wall carpeting in front of the fire; it is where I sometimes sleep, when the sun is high. I bring in blankets and pillows. We undress slowly; I let Ray take off my clothes. He touches my body, and I kiss his from head to foot. Then we lie down together and the sex is a wonder to him, as well as to me. I am careful not to hurt him.

Later, when he is asleep, I go for an automatic weapon in the attic. I load the clip carefully, making sure all the parts are well oiled, ready for use. Then I return to Ray's side and put the weapon under my pillow. Ray is exhausted; I stroke his head and whisper words that will cause him to sleep away the entire day. I suspect Yaksha will not come until the following night—a fresh night for a fresh slaughter. It would be his way. I know my gun will not stop him. I have only Krishna's promise to protect me. But what is the promise of a God I don't even know if I believe in?

Yet one thing is certain. If Krishna was not God, he was the most extraordinary human who ever lived. Even more powerful than all the vampires combined. I think of him as I lie beside Ray, and I wonder about my feelings of love for the boy. If they are just my longing for the face of Krishna hidden inside him. I do remember Krishna's face well. It was a face that would be impossible to forget even after five thousand years.

9

Once more, I go back. We left the area, Yaksha and I. We were quickly joined by two of the men from the village who had disappeared. They were vampires. I was a vampire. But that word did not exist then. I didn't know what I was, except somehow I was like Yaksha.

The horror and the wonder of it all.

My craving for blood did not come over me in the first days, and Yaksha must have told the others not to speak to me about it, because they did not. But I did notice that bright light bothered me. The rays of the midday sun were almost intolerable. This I understood. Because when we were growing up, I had noticed that Yaksha had a tendency to disappear in the middle of the day. It saddened me that I would never again enjoy a wonderful daytime sky.

Yet the nights, they became a thing of great beauty. For I could see in the dark better than I had been able to see in the day. I would look up at the moon and see that it was not the smooth orb we had all believed, but a pitted and scarred world with no air. Distant objects would appear before me as if only an arm's length away. I could see detail I had never imagined before: the pores of my skin; the multifaceted eyes of tiny insects. Sound, even on a supposedly silent plain, became a constant. I quickly became sensitive to the breathing patterns of different people. What each rhythm meant, how it corresponded to different emotions. My sense of smell took on an incredible vitality. With just a slight shift of the breeze the world was constantly bathed in new perfumes.

My newfound strength I loved most of all. I could leap to the top of the tallest tree, crumble huge boulders with a clap of my hands. I loved to chase the animals, especially the lions and tigers. They ran from me. They knew there was something inhuman about me.

But my blood hunger came over me quickly. On the fourth day I went to Yaksha and told him my chest was on fire and my heart was pounding in my ears. Honestly, I thought I was dying—I kept thinking about bleeding things. Yet I did not think of drinking blood, it was too impossible an idea. Even when Yaksha told me it was the only way to stop the pain, I pushed it out of my mind. Because even though I was no longer human, I wanted to pretend I was. When Yaksha had held me that long night, I felt myself die. Yet I imagined that I was alive as others were alive. But the life in me was not from this world. I could live off that life, but I could never give in to it. Yaksha told me I was sterile at the same time he told me about the blood. It made me cry for Lalita and Rama and wonder how they were doing without their Sita.

But I would not go to see them.

I would not let them see the monster I had become.

I feared I would make them vampires, too.

I resisted drinking another's blood, until pain was all I knew. I grew weak; I couldn't stop moaning. It was as if because I would not drink another's blood, then the thing Yaksha had put inside me would eat me alive. A month after my transformation, Yaksha brought me a half-conscious boy, with his neck veins already partially open, and ordered me to drink. How I hated him then for putting such temptation in front of me. How it rekindled in me my hatred for how he had taken me from Rama and Lalita. Yet my hate did not give me strength because it was not a pure thing. I needed Yaksha after he changed me, and need is a close kin of love. But I would not say I ever loved Yaksha; rather, I looked up to him because he was greater than I was. For a long time he was the only one to look up to—until Krishna.

Yet I drank the boy's blood. I fell upon him even as I swooned. And even though I resolved not to kill him, I couldn't stop drinking once I started. Then the boy was dead. I cried in horror as he took his last breath in my arms. But Yaksha just laughed. He said that once you killed, it was easy to kill again.

Yes, I hated him then because I knew he was right. After that, I killed many, and I grew to love it.

The years went by. We headed southeast. We never stopped moving. It never took that long for people in a village to realize we were dangerous. We came, we made friends—eventually we slew, and the rumors went before us. We also made more of our kind. The first vampire I created was a girl my age, with large dark eyes and hair like a waterfall made from the light of the midnight sky. I imagined she could become a friend, even though I took her against her will. By then Yaksha had told me what was necessary: the lifting out of my vein coming from my heart; the merger of her vein going back to the heart; the transfusion; the terror; the ecstasy. Her name was Mataji, and she never thanked me for what I did to her, but she stayed close in the years to come.

Making Mataji drained my strength, and it was several days and many victims later before I regained my full powers. It was the same for all of us except Yaksha. When he created another, he just grew stronger. I knew it was because it was his soul that fed us all. The yakshini embodied. The demon from the deep.

Yet there was kindness in him, but I couldn't understand its source. He was protective of all he created, and he was unusually nice to me. He never again told me that he loved me, however, but he did. His eyes were often on me. What was I supposed to do? The damned could not marry. God would not witness the union as we had been taught from the Vedas.

It was then, maybe after fifty years of being a vampire, that we began to hear stories about a man many said was the Veda incarnate. A man who was more than a man, perhaps Lord Vishnu himself. Each new village we plundered brought us another detail. His principal name was Krishna and he lived in the forests of Vrindavana near the Yumana River, with the cowherders and their milkmaids—the *gopis,* they were called. It was said this man, this Vasudeva—he had many names—was capable of slaying demons and granting bliss. His best friends were the five Pandava brothers, who had the reputation of being the incarnation of more minor deities. Arjuna, one of the brothers, had almost the fame of Krishna. He was said to be the son of the great god Indra, the lord of paradise. We did not doubt, from what we heard, that Arjuna was indeed a magnificent warrior.

Yaksha was intrigued. The rest of us vampires were as well, but few of us wanted to meet Krishna. Because even though our numbers by then were close to a thousand, we felt Krishna would not greet us with open arms, and if half the stories told about him and his friends were true, he might destroy us all. But Yaksha could not bear the thought that there was a man in the land more powerful than he. Because his reputation had grown great as well, although it was the notoriety of terror.

We set out for Vrindavana, all of us, and we marched openly, making no secret of our destination. The many mortals whom we passed seemed happy, for they believed our wandering herd of blood drinkers was doomed. I saw the gratitude in their faces and felt the fear in my heart. None of these people had personally met Krishna. Yet they believed in him. They simply trusted in the sound of his name. Even as we slew many of them, they called out to Krishna.

Of course Krishna knew we were coming; it required no omniscience on his part. Yaksha had a shrewd intellect, yet it was clouded by the arrogance his powers had given him. As we entered the forests of Vrindavana, all seemed calm. Indeed, the woods appeared deserted, even to us with acute hearing. But Krishna was only saving his attack until we were deep into his land. All of a sudden arrows began to fly toward us. Not a rain of them, but one at a time. Yet in quick succession and fired with perfect accuracy. Truly, not one of those arrows missed its target. They went through the hearts and heads of our kind. They never failed to kill that which Yaksha had told us could not be killed. And the most amazing thing is we could not catch the man who shot the arrows. We could not even see him, his *kavach,* his mystical armor, was that great.

Mataji was one of the first to fall, an arrow between her eyes.

Still, we were many, and it was going to take time even for the finest archer of all time to kill us. Yaksha drove us forward, as fast as we could go. Then the arrows began to strike only the rear of our contingent, and then they ceased altogether. It appeared that we had been able to outrun even Arjuna. But we had left many behind. Rebellion stirred against Yaksha. Most wanted to leave Vrindavana, if they knew which way to flee. For the first time Yaksha was losing command. But it was then, in those enchanted woods, that we came across what at first seemed to Yaksha a great boon. We ran into Radha, the chief of the gopis, Krishna's consort.

We had heard about Radha as well, whose name meant "longing." She was called this because she longed for Krishna even more than she desired to breathe. She was picking jasmines by the clear waters of the Yamuna when we came across her. We did not frighten her; she actually smiled when she saw us. Her beauty was extraordinary; I had never seen and never would see in five thousand years such an exquisite female. Her skin was remarkably fair; her face shone with the subtle radiance of moonlight. Her form was shapely. She moved as if in a joyful theater; each turn of her arm or bending of knees seemed to bring bliss. It was because each step she took, she took with the thought of Krishna. She was singing a song about him when we came upon her. In fact, the first words out of her mouth were to ask us if we wanted to learn it.

Yaksha immediately took her captive. She did not

try to hide her identity. We bound her wrists and ankles. I was put in charge of her while Yaksha sent several of our kind calling through the woods that we had Radha and that we were going to kill her unless Krishna agreed to meet Yaksha in single combat. It did not take Krishna long to respond. He sent Yudhishthira, Arjuna's brother, with a message. He would meet us at the edge of Vrindavana where we had entered the woods. If we did not know how to find it, Yudhishthira would show us the way. He had only two conditions. That we not harm Radha, and that he get to choose the form of combat. Yaksha sent Yudhishthira back saying that he accepted the challenge. It may have been that we should have first asked Yudhishthira which way to go. The woods were like a maze, and Radha was not talking. Yet she did not seem afraid. Occasionally she would glance my way and smile with such calm assurance that it was I who knew fear.

Yaksha was ecstatic. He did not believe any mortal could beat him at any form of combat. By such a pronouncement he appeared to discount the stories concerning Krishna's divine origin. Yet when I asked him about that, he did not answer me. He had a light in his eyes, though. He said that he had been born for this moment. Personally, I was fearful of a trick. Krishna had a reputation for being mischievous. Yaksha brushed aside my concerns. He would destroy Krishna, he said, then he would make Radha a vampire. She would be *his* consort. I did not feel jealous, I did not think it would happen.

Eventually we found our way back to the place where we had entered the forest. We remembered the spot because there was a huge pit in the ground. Apparently Krishna intended to use this pit when he challenged Yaksha. His people were gathered about it when we came out of the woods. Yet they made no attempt to attack us, although our numbers were roughly equal. I saw Arjuna, standing near his brothers, his mighty bow in his hands. When he looked my way and saw me holding on to Radha, he frowned and took an arrow into his hands and rubbed it to his chest. But he did nothing more. He was waiting for his master. We were all waiting. In that moment, even though I was not yet seventy years old, I felt as if I had waited since the dawn of creation to see this person. I who held captive his great jewel.

Krishna came out of the forest.

He was not a blue person as he was later to be depicted in paintings. Artists were to show him that way only because blue was symbolic of the sky, which to them seemed to stretch to infinity, and which was what Krishna was supposed to be in essence, the eternal infinite Brahman, above and beyond which there was nothing greater. He was a man such as all men I had seen, with two arms and two legs, one head above his shoulders, his skin the color of tea with milk in it, not as dark as most in India but not as light as my own. Yet there was no one like him. Even a glance showed me that he was special in a way I knew I would never fully comprehend. He walked out of the trees and all eyes followed him.

He was tall, almost as tall as Yaksha, which was unusual for those days when people seldom grew to over six feet. His black hair was long—one of his many names was *Keshava,* master of the senses, or long-haired. In his right hand he held a lotus flower, in his left his fabled flute. He was powerfully built; his legs long, his every movement bewitching. He seemed not to look at anyone directly, but only to give sidelong glances. Yet these were enough to send a thrill through the crowd, on both sides. He was impossible not to stare at, though I tried hard to turn away. For I felt as if he were placing a spell over me that I would never recover from. Yet I did manage to turn aside for an instant. It was when I felt the touch of a hand on my brow. It was Radha, my supposed enemy, comforting me with her touch.

"Krishna means love," she said. "But Radha means longing. Longing is older than love. I am older than he. Did you know that, Sita?"

I looked at her. "How did you know my name?"

"He told me."

"When?"

"Once."

"What else did he tell you about me?"

Her face darkened. "You do not want to know."

Krishna walked to the edge of the pit and gestured for his people to withdraw to the edge of the trees.

Only Arjuna remained with him. He nodded to Yaksha, who likewise motioned for our people to back up. But Yaksha wanted me near the pit with my hands not far from Radha's neck. The arrangement did not seem to bother Krishna. He met Yaksha not far from where I stood. Krishna did not look directly at Radha or me. Yet he was close enough so that I could hear him speak. His voice was mesmerizing. It was not so much the sound of his words, but the place from which they sprang. Their authority and power. And, yes, love, I could hear love even as he spoke to his enemy. There was such peace in his tone. With all that was happening, he was not disturbed. I had the feeling that for him it was merely a play. That we were all just actors in a drama he was directing. But I was not enjoying the part I had been selected for. I did not see how Yaksha could beat Krishna. I felt sure that this day would be our last.

Yet it was not day, but night, although the dawn was not far off.

"I have heard that Yaksha is the master of serpents," Krishna said. "That the sound of his flute intoxicates them. As you may have heard, I also play the flute. It is in my mind to challenge you to a combat of instruments. We will fill this pit with cobras, and you will sit at one end, and I will sit at the other, and we will each play for the control of the serpents. We will play for the life of Radha. You may play what you wish, and if the serpents strike me dead, so be it. You may keep Radha for your own pleasure. But if the serpents should bite you so many times that you die, or decide to surrender, then you must swear to me now that you will take a vow that I will ask you to take. Is this a reasonable challenge?"

"Yes," Yaksha said. His confidence leaped even higher, and I knew how strong Yaksha was with snakes. For I had watched many times while he had hypnotized snakes with the sound of his flute. It never surprised me because sometimes yakshinis were depicted as serpents, and I thought Yaksha was a snake at heart. In reality vampires have more in common with snakes than bats. A snake prefers to eat its victim alive.

I knew Yaksha could be bitten many times by a cobra and not die.

Krishna left it to our people to gather the cobras, which took time because there were none in the forests of Vrindavana itself. But vampires can work fast if they must, and travel far, and by the following evening the pit was filled with deadly snakes. Now the feeling in our group favored Yaksha. Few believed a mortal could survive for any length of time in the pit. It was then I saw that even though Krishna had impressed the vampires, they still thought of him as a man, an extraordinary man, true, but not as a divine being. They were anxious for the contest to begin.

I stayed with Radha throughout the day. I talked to her about Rama and Lalita. She told me that they had both passed out of this world, but that Rama's life had been noble and my daughter's had been happy. I did not ask how she knew these things, I simply believed her. I cried at her words. Radha tried to comfort me. All that are born die, she said. All who die are reborn. It is inevitable, Krishna had told her. She told me many things Krishna had said.

Finally, close to dark, Yaksha and Krishna climbed into the pit. Each carried a flute, nothing more. The people on both sides watched, but from a distance as Krishna had wanted. Only Radha and I stood close to the pit. There had to be a hundred snakes in that huge hole. They bit each other and more than a few were already being eaten.

Yaksha and Krishna sat at opposite ends of the pit, each with his back to the wall of earth. They began to play immediately. They had to; the snakes moved for each of them right away. But with the sound of the music, both melodies, the snakes backed off and appeared uncertain.

Now, Yaksha could play wonderfully, although his songs were always laced with sorrow and pain. His music was hypnotic; he could draw victims to feed on simply with his flute. But I realized instantly that his playing, for all its power, was a mere shadow next to Krishna's music. For Krishna played the song of life itself. Each note on his flute was like a different center in the human body. His breath through the notes on the flute was like the universal breath through the bodies of all people. He would play the third note on his flute and the third center in my body, at the navel, would vibrate with different emotions. The navel is the seat of jealousy and attachment, and of joy and generosity. I felt these as he played. When Krishna would blow through this hole with a heavy breath, I would feel as if everything that I had ever called mine had been stripped from me. But when he would change his breath, let the notes go long and light, then I would smile and want to give something to those around me. Such was his mastery.

His playing had the snakes completely bewildered. None would attack him. Yet Yaksha was able to keep the snakes at bay with his music as well, although he was not able to send them after his foe. So the contest went on for a long time without either side hurting the other. Yet it was clear to me Krishna was in command, as he was in control of my emotions. He moved to the fifth note on the flute, which stirred the fifth center in my body, at the throat. In that spot there are two emotions: sorrow and gratitude. Both emotions bring tears, one bitter, the other sweet. When Krishna lowered his breath, I felt like weeping. When he sang higher I also felt choked, but with thanks. Yet I did not know what I was thankful for. Not the outcome of the contest, surely. I knew then that Yaksha would certainly lose, and that the result could be nothing other than our extinction.

Even as the recognition of our impending doom crossed my mind, Krishna began to play the fourth note. This affected my heart; it affected the hearts of all gathered. In the heart are three emotions—I felt them then: love, fear, and hatred. I could see that an individual could only have one of the three at a time. When you were in love you knew no fear or hatred. When you were fearful, there was no possibility of love or hate. And when there was hate, there was only hate.

Krishna played the fourth note softly initially, so that a feeling of warmth swept both sides. This he did for a long time, and it seemed as if vampires and mortals alike stared across the clearing at one another and wondered why they were enemies. Such was the power of that one note, perfectly pitched.

Yet Krishna now pushed his play toward its climax. He lowered his breath, and the love in the gathering turned to hate. A restlessness went through the crowd, and individuals on both sides shifted this way and that as if preparing to attack. Then Krishna played the fourth note in a different way, and the hate changed to fear. And finally this emotion pierced Yaksha, who had so far remained unmoved by Krishna's flute. I saw him tremble—the worst thing he could do before a swarm of snakes. Because a serpent only strikes where there is fear.

The group of snakes began to crawl toward Yaksha.

He could have surrendered then, but he was a brave creature even if he was ruthless. He continued to play, now a frantic tune to drive away the snakes. At first it did slow them down, but Krishna did not tire. He continued on the fourth note, his breath quivering up and down through the hole, and at last a large snake slithered up to Yaksha. It bit him on the shin and held on fast with its teeth. Yaksha could not afford to set down his flute to throw it off. Then another snake came forward, and still another, until soon Yaksha was being bitten on every part of his body. He was the king of vampires, the son of a yakshini, yet even his system could absorb only so much venom. At last the flute fell from his hands and he swayed where he sat. I believe he tried to call out; I think he might have said my name. Then he toppled forward and the snakes began to eat him. I could not bear to watch.

But Krishna stood then and set his flute aside. He clapped his hands, and the snakes hurried off Yaksha's body. He climbed out of the pit and motioned to Arjuna. His best friend entered the deep hole and carried out Yaksha's body and dumped it on the ground not far from me. He was breathing, I could see that, but barely, soaked head to foot with black venom; it oozed out of the many wounds on his body.

I let Radha go. She hugged me before leaving. But she did not run to Krishna, but to the other women. Behind me I could hear the main body of the vampires shifting toward the woods, as if they planned to flee. Yet they waited still; they felt compelled to, I think, to see what Krishna would do next. Krishna ignored them. He gestured to me and came and knelt beside Yaksha. My feeling then was so peculiar. As I knelt beside Krishna, this being that would in all probability wipe me from the face of the earth, I felt as if I was under the umbrella of his protection. I watched as he put one of his beautiful hands on Yaksha's head.

"Will he live?" I asked.

Krishna surprised me with his question. "Do you want him to?"

My eyes strayed over the ruin of my old enemy and friend. "I want what you want," I whispered.

Krishna smiled, so serene. "The age is to change when I leave this world. Kali Yuga will begin. It will be a time of strife and short years for humanity. Your kind is for the most part tamasic—negative. Kali Yuga will be challenge enough for people without you on earth. Do you agree?"

"Yes. We cause only suffering."

"Then why do you go on, Sita?"

At his saying my name I felt so touched. "I just want to live, Lord."

He nodded. "I will let you live if you obey my command. If you never make another of your kind, you will have my grace, my protection."

I lowered my head. "Thank you, my Lord."

He gestured toward the other vampires. "Go stand with them. I must talk to your leader. His days are not over. They will not be over for a long time." I moved to leave, but Krishna stopped me. "Sita?"

I turned to look into his face one last time. It was as if I could see the whole universe in his eyes. Maybe he was God, maybe he was simply enlightened. I didn't care right then, in that blessed moment, I just loved him. Later, though, the love was to turn to hate, to fear. They seemed so opposite, the feelings, yet they were all one note on his flute. Truly he had stolen my heart.

"Yes, Lord?" I said.

He bid me lean close to his lips. "Where there is love, there is my grace," he whispered. "Remember that."

"I will try, my Lord."

I went and stood with the others. Krishna revived Yaksha and spoke softly in his ear. When Krishna was done, Yaksha nodded. Krishna bade him climb to his feet, and we saw that Yaksha's wounds were gone. Yaksha walked toward us.

"Krishna says we can go," he said.

"What did he tell you?" I asked.

"I cannot say. What did he tell you?"

"I cannot say."

Yet it was not long before I learned part of what Krishna had told Yaksha. Yaksha secretly began to execute each of the vampires. His acts did not stay secret long. I fled, we all did. But he hunted down the others, over the long years, even after Krishna was gone and Kali Yuga reigned. Yaksha chased them to the ends of the earth over the many centuries until there were none left that I knew of, except me. Yet he never came for me, and in the Middle Ages, as the Black Plague swept Europe, I heard that he was accused of being a witch, and also hunted down, by an entire army, and burned to ash in an old castle. I cried when the news came to me because even though he had stolen what I loved, he had in a sense created what I was. He was my lord as Krishna was my lord. I served both masters, light and darkness, both of which I had seen in Krishna's eyes. Even the devil does God's will.

I never made another vampire, but I never stopped killing.

10 ~~~

Ray stirs as the sun descends toward the western horizon. I sit by the fax machine on the small table at the end of my living room sofa, with the numbers Riley and Slim have provided for me. But I do not send Yaksha a message. It is not necessary. He is coming, I can feel him coming.

"Ray," I say. "It's time to get up and enjoy the night."

Ray sits up and yawns. He wipes the sleep from his eyes like a little boy. He checks the time and is amazed. "I slept away the entire day?" he asks.

"Yes," I say. "And now you have to go. I have decided. It is not safe for you here. Go to Pat. She loves you."

He throws aside the blankets and pulls on his pants. He comes and sits beside me and touches my arm. "I am not going to leave you."

"You cannot protect me. You can only get yourself killed."

"If I get killed, then I get killed. At least I will have tried."

"Brave words, foolish words. I can make you leave. I can tell you things about myself that will make you run out of here cursing my name."

He smiles. "I do not believe that."

I harden my tone, though it breaks my heart to treat him cruelly. But I have decided that my reasons for bringing him to my home are selfish. I must have him go, whatever it costs.

"Then listen to me," I say. "I lied to you last night even when I supposedly opened my heart to you. The first thing you must know is that your father is dead and that it was I, not Yaksha, who killed him."

Ray sits back, stunned. "You're not serious."

"I can show you where his body is buried."

"But you couldn't have killed him. Why? How?"

"I will answer your questions. I killed him because he called me into his office and tried to blackmail me with information he had dug up on me. He threatened to make it public. I killed him by crushing the bones of his chest."

"You couldn't do that."

"But you know that I can. You know what I am." I

reach over and pick up a small miniature of the Pyramid of Giza that stands on my living room table. "This piece was made for me out of solid marble by an artist in Egypt two hundred years ago. It is very heavy. You can feel it if you don't believe me."

Ray's eyes are dark. "I believe you."

"You should." I hold the piece in my right hand. I squeeze tight and it shatters to dust. Ray jumps back. "You should believe everything I tell you."

He takes a moment to collect himself. "You are a vampire."

"Yes."

"I knew there was something about you."

"Yes."

There is pain in his voice. "But you couldn't have killed my father."

"But I did. I killed him without mercy. I have killed thousands over the last five thousand years. I am a monster."

His eyes are moist. "But you would not do anything to hurt me. You want me to leave now because you do not want me to get hurt. You love me, I love you. Tell me you didn't kill him."

I take his hands in mine. "Ray, this is a beautiful world and it is a horrible world. Most people never see the horror that there is. For most that is fine. But you must look at it now. You must look deep into my eyes and see that I am not human, that I do inhuman things. Yes, I killed your father. He died in my arms.

He will not be coming home. And if you do not leave here, you will not return home, either. Then your father's dying wish will have been in vain."

Ray weeps. "He made a wish?"

"Not with words, but, yes. I picked up your picture and he cried. By then he knew what I was, though it was too late for him. He did not want me to touch you." I caress Ray's arms. "But it is not too late for you. Please go."

"But if you are so horrible why did you touch me, love me?"

"You remind me of someone."

"Who?"

"My husband, Rama. The night I was made a vampire, I was forced to leave him. I never saw him again."

"Five thousand years ago?"

"Yes."

"Are you really that old?"

"Yes. I knew Krishna."

"Hare Krishna?"

The moment is so serious, but I have to laugh. "He was not the way you think from what you see these days. Krishna was—there are no words for him. He was everything. It is he who has protected me all these years."

"You believe that?"

I hesitate, but it is true. Why can't I accept the truth? "Yes."

"Why?"

"Because he told me he would if I listened to him. And because it has been so. Many times, even with my great power, I should have perished. But I never did. God blessed me." I add, "And he cursed me."

"How did he curse you?"

Now there are tears in my eyes. "By putting me in this situation again. I cannot lose you again, my love, but I cannot keep you with me, either. Go now before Yaksha arrives. Forgive me for what I did to your father. He was not a bad man. He only wanted the money so that he could give it to you. I know he loved you very much."

"But——"

"Wait!" I interrupt. Suddenly I hear something, the note of a flute, flowing with the noise of the waves, a single note, calling me to it, telling me that it is already too late. "He is here," I whisper.

"What? Where?"

I stand and walk to the wide windows that overlook the sea. Ray stands beside me. Down by the ocean, where the waves crash against the rocks, stands a solitary figure dressed in black. His back is to us, but I see the flute in his hand. His song is sad, as always. I don't know if he plays for me or himself, but maybe it is for both of us.

"Is that him?" Rays asks.

"Yes."

"He's alone. We should be able to take him. Do you have a gun?"

"I have one under my pillow over there. But a gun will not stop him. Not unless he was riddled with bullets."

"Why are you giving up without a fight?"

"I am not giving up. I am going to talk to him."

"I'm coming with you."

I turn to Ray and rub the hair on his head. He feels so delicate to me. "No. You cannot come. He is less human than I am. He will not be interested in what a human has to say." I put my finger to his lips as he starts to protest. "Do not argue with me. I do not argue."

"I am not going to leave," he says.

I sigh. "It may be too late for that already. Stay then. Watch. Pray."

"To Krishna?"

"God is God. His name doesn't matter. But I think only he can help us now."

A few minutes later I stand ten feet behind Yaksha. The wind is strong, bitter. It seems to blow straight out of the cold sun which hangs like a bloated drop of blood over the hazy western horizon. The spray from the waves clings to Yaksha's long black hair like so many drops of dew. For a moment I imagine him a statue that has stood outside my home for centuries. Always, he has been in my life, even when he was not there. He has stopped playing his flute.

"Hello," I say to this person I haven't spoken to since the dawn of history.

"Did you enjoy my song?" he asks, his back still to me.

"It was sad."

"It is a sad day."

"The day is ending," I say.

He nods as he turns. "I want it to end, Sita."

The years have not changed his appearance. Why does that surprise me when they haven't changed mine? I don't know. Yet I scrutinize him more closely. A man has to learn something in so many years, I think. He cannot be the beast that he was. He smiles at my thought.

"The form changes, the essence remains the same," he says. "That is something Krishna told me about nature. But for us the form does not change."

"It is because we are unnatural."

"Yes. Nature abhors the invader. We are not welcome in this world."

"But you look well."

"I am not. I am tired. I wish to die."

"I don't," I say.

"I know."

"You tested me with Slim and his people. To see how hard I would fight."

"Yes."

"But I passed the test. I don't want to die. Leave here. Go do what you must. I want nothing to do with it."

Yaksha shakes his head sadly, and that is one

change in him—his sorrow. It softens him somehow, making his eyes less cold. Yet the sorrow scares me more than his wicked glee used to. Yaksha was always so full of life for a being that would later be labeled the undead.

"I would let you go if I could," he says. "But I cannot."

"Because of the vow you took with Krishna?"

"Yes."

"What were his words?"

"He told me that I would have his grace if I destroyed the evil I had created."

"I suspected as much. Why didn't you destroy me?"

"There was time, at least in my mind. He did not put a time limit on me."

"You destroyed the others centuries ago."

He watches me. "You are very beautiful."

"Thank you."

"It warmed my heart to know your beauty still existed somewhere in the world." He pauses. "Why do you ask these questions? You know I didn't kill you because I love you."

"Do you still love me?"

"Of course."

"Then let me go."

"I cannot. I am sorry, Sita, truly."

"Is it so important to you that you die in his grace?"

Yaksha is grave. "It is why I came into this world. The Aghoran priest did not call me, I came of my own will. I knew Krishna was here. I came to get away from where I was. I came so that when I died I would be in that grace."

"But you tried to destroy Krishna?"

Yaksha shrugs as if that is not important. "The foolishness of youth."

"Was he God? Are you sure? Can we be sure?"

Yaksha shakes his head. "Even that does not matter. What is God? It is a word. Whatever Krishna was we both know he was not someone we can disobey. It is that simple."

I gesture to the waves. "Then the line has been drawn. The sea meets the shore. The infinite tells the finite what is supposed to be. I accept that. But you are faced with a problem. You do not know what Krishna said to me."

"I do. I have watched you long. The truth is obvious. He told you not to make another of your kind, and he would protect you."

"Yes. It is a paradox. If you try to destroy me, you will go against his word. If you do not try, then you are damned."

Yaksha is not moved by my words. He is a step ahead of me; he always was. He points to the house with his flute. Ray continues to stand beside the window, watching us.

"I have watched you particularly close the last three days," he says. "You love this boy. You would not want to see him die."

My fear is a great and terrible thing in this moment. But I speak harshly. "If you use that as a threat to force me to destroy myself, then you will still lose Krishna's grace. It will be as if you struck me down with your own hands."

Yaksha does not respond with anger. Indeed, he does seem weary. "You misunderstand me. I will do nothing to you while you are protected by his grace. I will force you to do nothing." He gestures to the setting sun. "It takes a night to make a vampire. I am sure you remember. When the sun rises again, I will come back for you, for both of you. By then you should be done. Then you will be mine."

There is scorn in my voice. "You are a fool, Yaksha. The temptation to make another of our kind has come to me many times in the long years, and always I have resisted it. I will not forsake my protection. Face it, you are beaten. Die and return to the black hell from where you came."

Yaksha raises an eyebrow. "You know I am no fool, Sita. Listen."

He glances toward the house, at Ray, then raises the flute to his lips. He plays a single note, piercingly high. I shake with pain as the sound vibrates through my body. Behind us I hear glass break. No, not just glass. The window against which Ray is leaning. I turn in time to see him topple through the broken glass and plunge headfirst onto the concrete driveway sixty feet below. Yaksha grabs my arm as I move to run to him.

"I wish it did not have to be this way," he says.

I shake off his hand. "I have never loved you. You

may yet have grace before you die, but you will never have that."

He closes his eyes briefly. "So be it," he says.

I find Ray in a pool of blood and a pile of glass. His skull is crushed, his spine is broken. Incredibly, he is still conscious, although he does not have long to live. I roll him over on his back, and he speaks to me with blood pouring from his mouth.

"I fell," he says.

My tears are as cold as the ocean drops on my cheeks. I put my hand over his heart. "This is the last thing I wanted for you."

"Is he going to let you go?"

"I don't know, Ray. I don't know." I lean over and hug him and hear the blood in his lungs as his breath struggles to scrape past it. Just as the breath of his father struggled before it failed. I remember I told the man that I could not heal, that I could only kill. But that was only a half truth, I realize, even as I grasp the full extent of Yaksha's plan to destroy me. Once he used my fear to make me a vampire. Now he uses my love to force me to make another vampire. He is right, he is no fool. I cannot bear to watch Ray die knowing the power in my blood can heal even his fatal injuries.

"I wanted to save you," he whispers. He tries to raise a hand to touch me, but it falls back to the ground. I sit up and stare into his mortal eyes, trying to put love into them, where for so many years with so many other mortals I have only tried to put fear.

"I want to save you," I say. "Do you want me to save you?"

"Can you?"

"Yes. I can put my blood in your blood."

He tries to smile. "Become a vampire like you?"

I nod and smile through my tears. "Yes, you could become like me."

"Would I have to hurt people?"

"No. Not all vampires hurt people." I touch his ruined cheek. I haven't forgotten Yaksha's words about coming for both of us at dawn. "Some vampires love a great deal."

"I love . . ." His eyes slowly close. He cannot finish.

I lean over and kiss his lips. I taste his blood.

I will have to do more than taste it to help him.

"You are love," I say as I open both our veins.

11 ～～

Ray's sleep is deep and profound, as I expect. I have brought him back to the house, and laid him in front of a fire I built, and wiped away his blood. Not long after his transfusion, while still lying crumpled on the driveway, his breath had accelerated rapidly, and then ceased altogether. But it had not scared me, because the same had happened to me, and to Mataji, and many others. When it had started again, it was strong and steady.

His wounds vanished as if by magic.

I am weak from sharing my blood, very tired.

I anticipate that Ray will sleep away most of the night, and that Yaksha will keep his word and not return until dawn. I leave the house and drive in my

Ferrari to Seymour's place. It is not that late—ten o'clock. I do not want to meet his parents. They might suspect I have come to corrupt their beloved son. I go around the back and see Seymour through his bedroom window, writing on his computer. I scratch on his window with my hard nails and give him a scare. He comes over to investigate, however. He is delighted to see me. He opens the window and I climb inside. Contrary to popular opinion, I could have climbed in without being invited.

"It is so cool you are here," he says. "I have been writing about you all day."

I sit on his bed; he stays at his desk. His room is filled with science things—telescopes and such—but the walls are coated with the posters of classic horror films. It is a room I am comfortable in. I often go to the movies, the late shows.

"A story about me?" I ask. I glance at his computer screen, but he has returned to the word processor menu.

"Yes. Well, no, not really. But you inspired the story. It comes to me in waves. It's about this girl our age who's a vampire."

"I am a vampire."

He fixes his bulky glasses on his nose. "What?"

"I said, I am a vampire."

He glances at the mirror above his chest of drawers. "I can see your reflection."

"So what? I am what I say I am. Do you want me to drink your blood to prove it?"

"That's all right, you don't have to." He takes a deep breath. "Wow, I knew you were an interesting girl, but I never guessed . . ." He stops himself. "But I suppose that's not true, is it? I have been writing about you all along, haven't I?"

"Yes."

"But how is that possible? Can you explain that to me?"

"No. It's one of those mysteries. You run into them every now and then, if you live long enough."

"How old are you?"

"Five thousand years."

Seymour holds up his hand. "Wait, wait. Let's slow down here. I don't want to be a pest about this, and I sure don't want you to drink my blood, but before we proceed any further, I wouldn't mind if you showed me some of your powers. It would help with my research, you understand."

I smile. "You really don't believe me, do you? That's OK. I don't know if I want you to, not now. But I do want your advice." I lose my smile. "I am getting near the end of things now. An old enemy has come for me, and for the first time in my long life I am vulnerable to attack. You are the smart boy with the prophetic dreams. Tell me what to do."

"I have prophetic dreams?"

"Yes. Trust me or I wouldn't be here."

"What does this old enemy want? To kill you?"

"To kill both of us. But he doesn't want to die until I am gone."

"Why does he want to die?"

"He is tired of living."

"Been around for a while, I guess." Seymour thinks a moment. "Would he mind dying at the same time as you?"

"I'm sure that would be satisfactory. It might even appeal to him."

"Then that's the answer to your problem. Place him in a situation where he is convinced you're both goners. But arrange it ahead of time so that when you do push the button—or whatever you do—that only he is destroyed and not you."

"That's an interesting idea."

"Thank you. I was thinking of using it in my story."

"But there are problems with it. This enemy is extremely shrewd. It will not be easy to convince him that I am going to die with him unless it is pretty certain that I am going to die. And I don't want to die."

"There must be a way. There is always a way."

"What are you going to do in your story?"

"I haven't worked out that little detail yet."

"That detail is not little to me at the moment."

"I'm sorry."

"That's all right." I listen to his parents watching TV in the other room. They talk about their boy, his health. The mother is grief-stricken. Seymour watches me through his thick lenses.

"It's hardest on my mother," he says.

"The AIDS virus is not new. A form of it existed in

the past, not exactly the same as what is going around now, but close enough. I saw it in action. Ancient Rome, in its decline, was stricken with it. Many people died. Whole villages. That's how it was stopped. The mortality rate in certain areas was so high that there was no one left alive to pass it on."

"That's interesting. There is no mention of that in history books."

"Do not trust in your books too much. History is something that can only be lived, it cannot be read about. Look at me, I am history." I sigh. "The stories I could tell you."

"Tell me."

I yawn, something I never do. Ray has drained me more than I realized. "I don't have time."

"Tell me how you managed to survive the AIDS epidemic of the past."

"My blood is potent. My immune system is impenetrable. I have not just come here to seek your help, although you have helped me. I have come here to help you. I want to give you my blood. Not enough to make you a vampire, but enough to destroy the virus in your system."

He is intrigued. "Will that work?"

"I don't know. I have never done it before."

"Could it be dangerous?"

"Sure. It might kill you."

He hesitates only a moment. "What do I have to do?"

"Come sit beside me on the bed." He does so.

"Give me your arm and close your eyes. I am going to open up one of your veins. Don't worry, I have had a lot of practice with this."

"I can imagine." He lets his arm rest in my lap, but he does not close his eyes.

"What's the matter?" I ask. "Are you afraid I will try to take advantage of you?"

"I wish you would. It's not every day the school nerd has the most beautiful girl in the school sitting on his bed." He clears his throat. "I know that you're in a hurry, but I wanted to tell you something before we begin."

"What's that?"

"I wanted to thank you for being my friend and letting me play a part in your story."

I think of Krishna, always of him, how he stood near me and I saw the whole universe as his play. "Thank you, Seymour, for writing about me." I lean over and kiss his lips. "If I die tonight, at least others will know I once lived." I stretch out my nails. "Close your eyes. You do not want to watch this."

I place a measured amount of blood inside him. His breath quickens, it burns, but not so fast or hot as Ray's had. Yet, like Ray, Seymour quickly falls into a deep slumber. I turn off his computer and put out the light. There is a blanket on the bed that looks as if it was knitted by his mother, and I cover him with it. Before I leave, I put my palm on his forehead and listen and feel as deep as my senses will allow.

The virus, I am almost sure of this, is gone.

I kiss him once more before I leave.

"Give me credit if you get your story published," I whisper in his ear. "Or else there will be no sequels."

I return to my car.

Giving out so much blood, taking none back in return.

I feel weaker than I have in centuries.

"There will be no sequels," I repeat to myself.

I start the car. I drive into the night.

I have work to do.

12 ～

Seymour has given me an idea. But even with his inspiration, and mine, even if everything goes exactly as planned, the chances of it working are fifty-fifty at best. In all probability much less than that. But at least the plan gives me hope. For myself and Ray. He is like my child now, as well as my lover. I cannot stand the thought that he is to be snuffed out so young. He was wrong to say I would give up without a fight. I fight until the end.

There is a concept NASA is entertaining to launch huge payloads into space. It is called Orion; the idea is revolutionary. Many experts, in fact, say it won't work in practice. Yet there are large numbers of respected physicists and engineers who believe it is the wave of the future in space transport. Essentially it involves constructing a huge heavily plated platform with cannons on the bottom that can fire miniature nuclear bombs. It is believed that the shock waves from the blasts of the bombs detonating—if their timing and power is perfectly balanced—can lift the platform steadily into the sky, until eventually escape velocity is achieved. The advantage of this idea over traditional rockets is that tremendous tonnage could be shot into space. The primary problem is obvious: who wants to strap themselves atop a platform that is going to have nuclear bombs going off beneath it? Of course, I would enjoy such a ride. Extreme radiation bothers me no more than a sunny day.

Even with my great resources, I do not have a nuclear bomb at my disposal. But the idea of the Orion project inspires a plan in me. Seymour hit the nail on the head when he said Yaksha must be placed in a situation where he thinks all three of us will perish. That will satisfy Yaksha. He will then go to Krishna believing all vampires are destroyed. I theorize that I can build my own Orion with dynamite and a heavy steel platform, and use it to allow Ray and me to escape while a secondary blast kills Yaksha.

This is how I see the details. I let Yaksha into my house. I tell him that I will not fight him, that we can all go out together in one big blast. I know the possibility will entice Yaksha. We can sit in the living room around a crate of dynamite. I can even let

Yaksha light the fuse. He will see that the bomb is big enough to kill us all.

But what he will not see is the six inches of steel sheeting under the carpet beneath my chair and Ray's. Our *two* chairs will be bolted to the steel sheet— through the carpet. The chairs will be part of the metal plate—one unit. Yaksha will not see a smaller bomb beneath the floor of the plate. This bomb I will detonate, before Yaksha's fuse burns down. This bomb will blast my amateur Orion toward the wide skylights in my ceiling. The shock wave from it will also trigger the larger bomb.

Simple. Yes? There are problems, I know.

The blast from the hidden bomb will trigger the larger bomb before we can fly clear. I estimate that the two bombs should go off almost simultaneously. But Ray and I need rise up only fifteen feet on our Orion. Then the blast from the larger bomb should propel us through the skylights. If the two bombs are more than fifteen feet apart—ideally twice that distance—then the shock wave from the hidden bomb should not get to the larger bomb before we have achieved our fifteen feet elevation.

Our heads will heal quickly after we smash through the skylights as long as we are in one piece.

The physics are simple in theory, but in practice they are filled with the possibility for limitless error. For that reason I figure Ray and I will be dead before sunrise. But any odds are good odds for the damned, and I will play them out as best I can.

I stop at a phone booth and call my primary troubleshooter in North America. I tell him I need dynamite and thick sheets of steel in two hours. Where can I get them? He is used to my unusual requests. He says he'll call back in twenty minutes.

Fifteen minutes later he is back on the line. He sounds relieved because he knows it's not good to bring me disappointing information. He says there is a contractor in Portland who carries both dynamite and thick steel plating. Franklin and Sons—they build skyscrapers. He gives me the address of their main warehouse and I hang up. Portland is eighty miles away. The time is ten-fifty.

I sit in my car outside the warehouse at a quarter to midnight, listening to the people inside. The place is closed, but there are three security men on duty. One is in the front in a small office watching TV. The other two are in back smoking a joint. Since I have spent a good part of the night thinking about Krishna, hoping he will help me, I am not predisposed to kill these three. I climb out of my car.

The locked doors cause me no problem. I am upon the stoned men in the back before they can blink. I put them to sleep with moderate blows to the temples. They'll wake up, but with bad headaches. Unfortunately, the guy watching TV has the bad luck to check on his partners as I knock them out. He draws his gun when he sees me, and I react instinctively. I kill him much the same way I killed Ray's father, crushing the bones in his chest with a violent kick. I drink a belly full of his blood before he draws his last breath. I am still weak.

The dynamite is not hard for me to find with my sensitive nose. It is locked in a safe near the front of the building, several crates of thick red sticks. There are detonator caps and fuses. Already I have decided I will not be taking my car back to Mayfair tonight. I will need a truck from the warehouse to haul the steel sheets. The metal is not as thick I wish; I will have to weld several layers together. I find a welding set to take with me.

There are actually several suitable trucks parked inside the warehouse, the keys conveniently left in the ignitions. I load up and back out of the warehouse. I park my Ferrari several blocks away. Then I am on the road back home.

It is after two when I reenter Mayfair. Ray is sitting by the fire as I come through my front door. He has changed. He is a vampire. His teeth are not longer, or anything silly like that. But the signs are there—gold specks deep in his once uniformly brown eyes; a faint transparency to his tan skin; a grace to his movements no mortal could emulate. He stands when he sees me.

"Am I alive?" he asks innocently.

I do not laugh at the question. I am not sure if the answer is something as simple as yes or no. I step toward him.

"You are with me," I say. "You are the same as me. When you met me, did you think I was alive?"

"Yes."

"Then you are alive. How do you feel?"

"Powerful. Overwhelmed. My eyes, my ears—are yours this way?"

"Mine are more sensitive. They become more and more sensitive with time. Are you scared?"

"Yes. Is he coming back?"

"Yes."

"When?"

"At dawn."

"Will he kill us?"

"He wants to."

"Why?"

"Because he feels we are evil. He feels an obligation to destroy us before he leaves the planet."

Ray frowns, testing his new body, its vibrancy. "Are we evil?"

I take his hands and sit him down. "We don't have to be. Soon you will begin to crave blood, and the blood will give you strength. But to get blood you don't need to kill. I will show you how."

"You said he wants to leave this planet. He wants to die?"

"Yes. He is tired of life. It happens—our lives have been so long. But life does not tire me." I am so emotional around Ray, it amazes me. "I have you to inspire me."

He smiles, but it is a sad smile. "It was a sacrifice for you to save me."

He takes my breath away. "How did you know?"

"When I was dying, I could see you were afraid to

175

give me your blood. What happens when you do? Does it make you weak?"

I hug him, glad that I can squeeze his body with all my strength and not break his bones. "Don't worry about me. I saved you because I wanted to save you."

"Is my father really dead?"

I let go of him, look into his eyes. "Yes."

He has trouble looking at me. Even though he is a vampire now, a predator. Even though his thought processes have begun to alter. He didn't protest when I told him about the blood-drinking. But his love for his father goes deeper than blood.

"Was it necessary?" he asked.

"Yes."

"Did he suffer?"

"No, less than a minute."

"I am sorry."

He finally raises his eyes. "You gave me your blood out of guilt as well."

I nod. "I had to give something back after what I had taken."

He puts a hand to his head. He doesn't completely forgive me but he understands, and for that I am grateful. He still misses his father. "We won't talk about it," he says.

"That is fine." I stand. "We have much to do. Yaksha is returning at dawn. We cannot destroy him with brute force, even with our combined strengths. But we might be able to trick him. We will talk as we work."

He stands. "You have a plan?"

"I have more than a plan. I have a rocket ship."

Welding the sheets of metal together so that we have six inches of protection does not take long. I work outside with the arc gun so that Yaksha will not notice the smell when he enters the house. He will have to come into the house since I won't go out to him. Cutting a huge rectangle in the floor to accommodate the metal plate, however, takes a lot of time. I fret as the hours slip by. Ray is not much help because he has not acquired my expertise in everything yet. Finally I tell him to sit and watch. He doesn't mind. His eyes are everywhere, staring at common objects, seeing in them things he never imagined before. A vampire on acid, I call him. He laughs. It is good to hear laughter.

As I work, I do not *feel* Yaksha in the area.

It is fortunate.

My speed picks up when I bolt the two chairs to the plate and recover the plate with carpet. Here I do not have to work so carefully; the skirts of the chairs cover much. When I am done, the living room appears normal. I plan to use an end table to hide the detonator to the bomb I will strap beneath the steel plate. I bore a long hole through the table and slip in a metal rod that goes through to the metal plate. I hide the tip of the rod under a lamp base. I place a blasting cap at the bottom end of it. When the time comes, I will hit the top of the small table, the rod will crush the blasting cap, and the first bomb will go off, sending us flying.

The other bomb should go off as well, almost immediately. I keep coming back to that point in my mind because it is the central weakness in my plan. I hope we will be high enough to take the shock from the second bomb from below so the plate will protect us.

Attaching the bomb beneath the plate takes only minutes. I use twenty sticks of dynamite, tightly bound. I place fifty sticks, a whole crate, beside the fireplace in the living room, next to the most comfortable chair in the house. That seat I will offer Yaksha. We will live or die depending on how accurate my calculations are, and how well we play our parts in front of Yaksha. That is the other serious weakness in my plan; that Yaksha will sense something amiss. For that reason I have instructed Ray to say little, or nothing at all. But I am confident I can lie to Yaksha. I lie as effortlessly as I tell the truth, perhaps more easily.

Ray and I sit in our special flight chairs and talk. The bomb in the crate sits thirty feet away, directly in front of us. Above us I have opened the skylights. The cold night air feels good for once. Even with them open, we will still strike glass as we rocket by. I warn Ray, but he is not worried.

"I have already died once today," he says.

"You must have had your nose pressed against the glass to fall with it."

"I didn't until just before he raised his flute."

I nod. "He glanced at the house then. He must have

pulled you forward with the power of his eyes. He can do that. He can do many things."

"He has more power than you?"

"Yes."

"Why is that?"

"He's the original vampire." I glance at the time— an hour to dawn. "Would you like to hear the story of his birth?"

"I would like to hear all your stories."

I smile. "You sound like Seymour. I visited him tonight while you slept. I gave him a present. I will tell you about it another time."

I pause and take a breath. I need it for strength. The simple work of a terrorist has exhausted me. Where to begin the tale? Where will I end it? It doesn't seem right that it could all be over in an hour. *Right*—what a word choice for a vampire to make. I who have violated every injunction of the Vedas and the Bible and every other holy book on earth. Death never comes at the *right* time, despite what mortals believe. Death always comes like a thief.

I tell Ray of the birth of Yaksha, and how he in turn made me a vampire. I talk to him about meeting Krishna, but here my words fail me. I do not weep, I do not rave. I simply cannot talk about him. Ray understands; he encourages me to tell him about my life in another era.

"Were you in Ancient Greece?" he asks. "I was always fascinated by that culture."

I nod. "I was there for a long time. I knew Socrates

and Plato and Aristotle. Socrates recognized me as something inhuman, but I didn't scare him. He was fearless, that man. He laughed as he drank the poison he was sentenced to drink." I shake my head at the memory. "The Greeks were inquisitive. There was one young man—Cleo. History does not remember him, but he was as brilliant as the others." My voice falters again. "He was dear to me. I lived with him for many years."

"Did he know you were a vampire?"

I laugh. "He thought I was a witch. But he liked witches."

"Tell me about him," Ray says.

"I met Cleo during the time of Socrates. I had just returned to Greece after being away for many years. That's my pattern. I stay in one place only as long as my youth, my constant youth, doesn't become suspicious. When I returned to Athens, no one remembered me. Cleo was one of the first people I encountered. I was walking in the woods when I found him helping to deliver a baby. In those days that was unheard of. Only women were present at births. Even though he was covered with blood and obviously busy, he took an immediate liking to me. He asked me to help him, which I did, and when the child was born, he handed it to the mother and we went for a walk. He explained that he had worked out a better way to deliver babies and had wanted to test his theories. He also admitted that he was the father of the infant, but that was not important to him.

"Cleo was a great doctor, but he was never recognized by his peers. He was ahead of his time. He refined the technique of the Caesarean delivery. He experimented with magnets and how they could restore ailing organs: the positive pole of the magnet to stimulate an organ, the negative pole to pacify it. He had an understanding of how the aromas of certain flowers could affect health. He was also the first chiropractor. He was always adjusting people's bodies, cracking their necks and backs. He tried to adjust me once and sprained his wrists. You can see why I liked him."

I went on to explain how I knew Cleo for many years, and spoke of his one fatal flaw: his obsession with seducing the wives of Athens' powerful men. How he was eventually caught in bed with the wife of an important general, and beheaded with a smile on his face, while many of the women of Athens wept. Wonderful Cleo.

I talk of a life I had as an English duchess in the Middle Ages. What it was like to live in a castle. My words bring back the memories. The constant drafts. The stone walls. The roaring fires—at night, how black those nights could be. My name was Melissa and in the summer months I would ride a white horse through the green countryside and laugh at the advances made to me by the knights in shining armor. I even accepted a couple of offers to jostle, offers the men later regretted making.

I speak of a life in the South during the American

Civil War. The burning and pillaging of the Yankees as they stormed across Mississippi. A note of bitterness enters my voice, but I do not tell Ray everything. Not how I was abducted by a battalion of twenty soldiers and tied at the neck with a rope and forced to grovel through a swamp, while the men joked about what pleasure I would give them come sunset. I do not want to scare Ray, so I do not explain how each of those men died, how they screamed, especially the last ones, as they tried to flee from the swamp in the dark, from the swift white hands that tore off their limbs and crushed their skulls.

Finally I tell him of how I was in Cape Canaveral when Apollo 11 was launched toward the moon. How proud I was of humanity then, that they had finally reclaimed the adventurous spirit they had known so well in their youth. Ray takes joy in my pleasure of the memory. It makes him forget the horror that awaits us, which is part of the reason I share the story.

"Did you ever want to go to the moon?" he asks.

"Pluto. Much farther from the sun, you know. More comfortable for a vampire."

"Did you grieve when Cleo died?"

I smile, although there is suddenly a tear in my eye. "No. He lived the life he wanted. Had he lived too long, he would have begun to bore himself."

"I understand."

"Good," I say.

But Ray doesn't really understand. He misconstrues the sentiment I show. My tear is not for Cleo. It is for my long life, the totality of it, all the people and places that are a part of it. Such a rich book of history to slam shut and store away in a forgotten corner. I grieve for all the stories I will never have a chance to tell Seymour and Ray. I grieve for the vow I have broken. I grieve for Yaksha and the love I could never give him. Most of all I grieve for my soul because even though I do, finally, believe that there is a God, and that I have met him, I do not know if he has given me an *immortal* soul, but only one that was to last me as long as my body lasted. I do not know if when the last page of my book is closed, that will be the end of me.

Darkness approaches from outside.

I feel no light inside me strong enough to resist it.

"He is coming," I say.

13 ⌁

There is a knock at the door. I call out to come in. He enters; he is alone, dressed in black, a cape, a hat—he makes a stunning figure. He nods and I gesture for him to take the chair across from us. He has not brought his flute. He sits in the chair near the crate of dynamite and smiles at both of us. But there is no joy in the smile, and I think he truly does regret what is about to happen. Outside, behind us through the broken windows, a hint of light enters the black sky. Ray sits silently staring at our visitor. It is up to me to make conversation.

"Are you happy?" I ask.

"I have known happiness at times," Yaksha says. "But it has been a long time."

"But you have what you want," I insist. "I have broken my vow. I have made another evil creature, another thing for you to destroy."

"I feel no compulsions these days, Sita, except to rest."

"I want to rest as well."

He raises an eyebrow. "You said you wanted to live?"

"It is my hope there will be life for me after this life is over. I assume that is your hope as well. I assume that is why you are going to all this trouble to wreck my night."

"You always had a way with words."

"Thank you."

Yaksha hesitates. "Do you have any last words?"

"A few. May I decide how we die?"

"You want us to die together?"

"Of course," I say.

Yaksha nods. "I prefer it that way." He glances at the crate of dynamite beside him. "You have made us a bomb, I see. I like bombs."

"I know. You can be the one to light it. You see the fuse there, the lighter beside it? Go ahead, old friend, strike the flame. We can burn together." I lean forward. "Maybe we should have burned a long time ago."

Yaksha picks up the lighter. He considers Ray. "How do you feel, young man?"

"Strange," Ray says.

"I would set you free if I could," Yaksha says. "I would leave you both alone. But it has to end, one way or the other."

This is a Yaksha I have never heard before. He never explained himself to anyone.

"Sita has told me your reasons," Ray says.

"Your father is dead," Yaksha says.

"I know."

Yaksha pulls his thumb across the lighter and stares at it. "I never knew my father."

"I saw him once," I say. "Ugly bastard. Are you going to do it or do you want me to do it?"

"Are you so anxious to die?" Yaksha asks.

"I never could wait for the excitement to begin," I say sarcastically.

He nods and moves the flame to the end of the fuse. It begins to fizzle, it begins to shorten—quickly. There are three minutes of time coiled in that combustible string. Yaksha sits back in his chair.

"I had a dream as I walked by the ocean tonight," he says. "Listening to the sound of the waves, it seemed I entered a dimension where the water was singing a song that no one had ever heard before. A song that explained everything in the creation. But the magic of the song was that it could never be recognized for what it was, not by any living soul. If it was, if the truth was brought out into the open and discussed, then the magic would die and the waters would evaporate. And that is what happened in my dream as this realization came to me. I came into the world. I killed all the creatures the waters had given life to, and then one day I woke up and realized I had been listening to a song. Just a sad song."

"Played on a flute?" I ask.

The fuse burns.

There is no reason for me to delay. Yet I do.

His dream moves me.

"Perhaps," Yaksha says softly. "In the dream the ocean vanished from my side. I walked along an endless barren plain of red dust. The ground was a dark red, as if a huge being had bled over it for centuries and then left the sun to parch dry what the being had lost."

"Or what it had stolen from others," I say.

"Perhaps," Yaksha says again.

"What does this dream mean?" I ask.

"I was hoping you could tell me, Sita."

"What can I tell you? I don't know your mind."

"But you do. It is the same as yours."

"No."

"Yes. How else could I know your mind?"

I tremble. His voice has changed. He is alert, he always was, to everything that was happening around him. I was a fool to think I could trick him. Yet I do not reach for the metal rod that will detonate the bomb. I try to play the fool a little longer. I speak.

"Maybe your dream means that if we stay on earth,

and once more multiply, then we will make a waste-land of this world."

"How would we multiply this late in the game?" he asks. "I told you you can have no children. Krishna told you something similar." It is his turn to lean forward. "What else did he tell you, Sita?"

"Nothing."

"You are lying."

"No."

"Yes." With his left hand he reaches for the burning fuse, his fingers hovering over the sparks as if he intends to crush them. Yet he lets the countdown continue. "You cannot trick me."

"And how do I trick you, Yaksha?"

"You are not waiting to die. I see it in your eyes."

"Really?"

"They are not like my eyes."

"You are a vampire," I say. Casually, as if I am stretching, I move my hand toward the lamp stand. "You can't look in a mirror. There would be nothing there. What do you know about your own eyes?" I joke, of course. I am one bundle of laughs.

He smiles. "I am happy to see time has not destroyed your wit. I hope it has not destroyed your reason. You are quick. I am quicker. You can do nothing that I cannot stop." He pauses. "I suggest you stop."

My hand freezes in midair. *Damn*, I think. He knows, of course he knows.

"I cannot remember what he said," I say.

"Your memory is perfect, as is mine."

"Then you tell me what he said."

"I cannot. He whispered in your ear. He did that so that I would not hear. He knew I was listening, even though I was lying there with the venom in my veins. Yes, I heard your original vow to him. But he did not want me to hear the last part. He would have had his reasons, I'm sure, but the time for those reasons must be past. We are both going to die in a few seconds. Did he make you take a second vow?"

The fuse burns.

"No."

Yaksha sits up. "Did he say anything about me?"

Shorter and shorter it burns.

"No!"

"Why won't you answer my question?"

The truth bursts out of me. I have wanted to say it for so long. "Because I hate you!"

"Why?"

"Because you stole away my love, my Rama and Lalita. You steal my love away now, when I have finally found it again. I will hate you for eternity, and if that is not enough to stop you from being in his grace, then I will hate him as well." I point to Ray. "Let him go. Let him live."

Yaksha is surprised. I have stunned the devil. "You love him. You love him more than your own life."

There is only pain in my chest. The fourth center, the fourth note. It is as if it is off key. "Yes."

Yaksha's tone softens. "Did he tell you something about love?"

I nod, weeping, I feel so helpless. "Yes."

"What did he tell you?"

"He said, where there is love, there is my grace." The sound of his flute is too far away. There is no time to be grateful for what I have been given in my long life. I feel as if I will choke on my grief. I can only see Ray, my lover, my child, all the years he will be denied. He looks at me with such trusting eyes, as if somehow I will still manage to save him. "He told me to remember that."

"He told me the same thing." Yaksha pauses to wonder. "It must be true." He adds casually, "You and your friend can go."

I look up. "What?"

"You broke your vow because you love this young man. It is the only reason you broke it. You must still have Krishna's grace. You only became a vampire to protect Rama and your child. You must have had his grace from the beginning. That is why he showed you such kindness. I did not see that till now. I cannot harm you. He would not wish me to." Yaksha glances at the burning fuse. "You had better hurry."

The sparks of the short fuse are like the final sands of an hourglass.

I grab Ray's hand and leap up and pull him toward

the front door. I do not open the door with my hand. I kick it open; the wrong way. The hinges rupture, the wood splinters. The night air is open before us. I shove Ray out ahead of me.

"Run!" I shout.

"But—"

"Run!"

He hears me, finally, and dashes for the trees. I turn, I don't know why. The chase is over and the race is won. There is no reason to tempt fate. What I do now, it is the most foolish act of my life. I stride back into the living room. Yaksha stares out at the dark sea. I stand behind him.

"You have ten seconds," he says.

"Hate and fear and love are all in the heart. I felt that when he played his flute." I touch his shoulder. "I don't just hate you. I didn't just fear you."

He turns and looks at me. He smiles; he always had a devilish grin.

"I know that, Sita," he says. "Goodbye."

"Goodbye."

I leap for the front door. I am outside, thirty feet off the front porch, when the bombs go off. The power of the shock wave is extraordinary even for me to absorb. It lifts me up, and for a few moments it is as if I can fly. But it does not set me down softly. At one point in my trajectory fate makes me a marksman's prized bird. An object hot and sharp pierces me from behind.

It goes through my heart. A stake.

I land in a ball of agony. The night burns behind me. My blood sears as it pours from the wound in my chest. Ray is beside me, asking me what he should do. I writhe in the dirt, my fingers clawing into the earth. But I do not want to go into the ground, no, not after walking on it for so long. I try to get the words out—it is not easy. I see I have been impaled by the splintered leg of my piano bench.

"Pull it out," I gasp.

"The stick?" It is the first stupid thing I have heard Ray say.

I turn my front to him. "Yes."

Ray grabs the end of the leg. The wood is literally flaming, although it has passed through my body. He yanks hard. The stick breaks; he has got half of it. The other half is still in my body. Too bad for me. I close my eyes for an instant and see a million red stars. I blink and they explode as if the universe has ended. There remains only red light everywhere. The color of sunset, the color of blood. I find myself settling onto my back. My head rolls to one side. Cool mud touches my cheek. It warms as my blood pours from my mouth and puddles around my head. A red stain, almost black in the fiery night, spreads down my beautiful blond hair. Ray weeps. I look at him with such love I honestly feel I see Krishna's face.

It is not the worst way to die.

"Love you," I whisper.

He hugs me. "I love you, Sita."

So much love, I think as I close my eyes and the pain recedes. There must be so much grace, so much protection for me if Krishna meant what he said. Of course I believe he meant it. I do believe in miracles.

I wonder if I will die, after all.

TO BE CONTINUED . . .

Look for Christopher Pike's

Remember Me 2: The Return

Coming in September 1994

About the Author

CHRISTOPHER PIKE was born in Brooklyn, New York, but grew up in Los Angeles, where he lives to this day. Prior to becoming a writer, he worked in a factory, painted houses, and programmed computers. His hobbies include astronomy, meditating, running, playing with his nieces and nephews, and making sure his books are prominently displayed in local bookstores. He is the author of *Last Act*, *Spellbound*, *Gimme a Kiss*, *Remember Me*, *Scavenger Hunt*, *Final Friends* 1, 2, and 3, *Fall into Darkness*, *See You Later*, *Witch*, *Die Softly*, *Bury Me Deep*, *Whisper of Death*, *Chain Letter 2: The Ancient Evil*, *Master of Murder*, *Monster*, *Road to Nowhere*, *The Eternal Enemy*, *The Immortal*, *The Wicked Heart*, and *The Midnight Club*, and *The Last Vampire*, all available from Archway Paperbacks. *Slumber Party*, *Weekend*, *Chain Letter*, and *Sati*—an adult novel about a very unusual lady—are also by Mr. Pike.

FEAR STREET®

R.L. Stine

- ☐ THE NEW GIRL......................................74649-9/$3.99
- ☐ THE SURPRISE PARTY........................73561-6/$3.99
- ☐ THE OVERNIGHT.................................74650-2/$3.99
- ☐ MISSING..69410-3/$3.99
- ☐ THE WRONG NUMBER.........................69411-1/$3.99
- ☐ THE SLEEPWALKER..............................74652-9/$3.99
- ☐ HAUNTED..74651-0/$3.99
- ☐ HALLOWEEN PARTY.............................70243-2/$3.99
- ☐ THE STEPSISTER..................................70244-0/$3.99
- ☐ SKI WEEKEND......................................72480-0/$3.99
- ☐ THE FIRE GAME...................................72481-9/$3.99
- ☐ LIGHTS OUT..72482-7/$3.99
- ☐ THE SECRET BEDROOM........................72483-5/$3.99
- ☐ THE KNIFE...72484-3/$3.99
- ☐ THE PROM QUEEN.................................72485-1/$3.99
- ☐ FIRST DATE...73865-8/$3.99
- ☐ THE BEST FRIEND.................................73866-6/$3.99
- ☐ THE CHEATER......................................73867-4/$3.99
- ☐ SUNBURN..73868-2/$3.99
- ☐ THE NEW BOY......................................73869-0/$3.99
- ☐ THE DARE..73870-4/$3.99
- ☐ BAD DREAMS.......................................78569-9/$3.99
- ☐ DOUBLE DATE ....78570-2/$3.99
- ☐ Fear Street Saga #1:THE BETRAYAL ....86831-4/$3.99
- ☐ Fear Street Saga #2:THE SECRET.............86832-2/$3.99
- ☐ Fear Street Saga #3: THE BURNING...........86833-0/$3.99
- ☐ CHEERLEADERS: THE FIRST EVIL.............75117-4/$3.99
- ☐ CHEERLEADERS: THE SECOND EVIL...........75118-2/$3.99
- ☐ CHEERLEADERS: THE THIRD EVIL.............75119-0/$3.99
- ☐ SUPER CHILLER: PARTY SUMMER...........72920-9/$3.99
- ☐ THE THRILL CLUB.................................78581-8/$3.99